TENNESSEE
SLAVE
NARRATIVES

A Folk History of Slavery in Tennessee
from Interviews with Former Slaves

* * *

Typewritten records prepared by
THE FEDERAL WRITERS' PROJECT
1936-1938

* * *

Published in cooperation with
THE LIBRARY OF CONGRESS

APPLEWOOD BOOKS
Bedford, Massachusetts

The LIBRARY
of CONGRESS

A portion of the proceeds from the sale
of this book is donated to the Library of
Congress, which holds the original Slave
Narratives in its collection.

Thank you for purchasing an Applewood book.
Applewood reprints America's lively classics
--books from the past that are still of
interest to modern readers. For a free copy
of our current catalog, write to:

Applewood Books
P.O. Box 365
Bedford, MA 01730

ISBN 1-55709-024-6

FOREWORD

More than 140 years have elapsed since the ratification of the Thirteenth Amendment to the U.S. Constitution declared slavery illegal in the United States, yet America is still wrestling with the legacy of slavery. One way to examine and understand the legacy of the 19th Century's "peculiar institution" in the 21st century is to read and listen to the stories of those who actually lived as slaves. It is through a close reading of these personal narratives that Americans can widen their understanding of the past, thus enriching the common memory we share.

The American Folklife Center at the Library of Congress is fortunate to hold a powerful and priceless sampling of sound recordings, manuscript interviews, and photographs of former slaves. The recordings of former slaves were made in the 1930s and early 1940s by folklorists John A. and Ruby T. Lomax, Alan Lomax, Zora Neale Hurston, Mary Elizabeth Barnicle, John Henry Faulk, Roscoe Lews, and others. These aural accounts provide the only existing sound of voices from the institution of slavery by individuals who had been held in bondage three generations earlier. These voices can be heard by visiting the web site http://memory.loc.gov/ammem/collections/voices/. Added to the Folklife Center collections, many of the narratives from manuscript sources, which you find in this volume, were collected under the auspices of the United States Works Progress Administration (WPA), and were known as the slave narrative collection. These transcripts are found in the Library of Congress Manuscript Division. Finally, in addition to the Folklife Center photographs, a treasure trove of Farm Security Administration (FSA) photographs (including those of many former slaves) reside in the Prints and Photographs Division here at the nation's library. Together, these primary source materials on audio tape, manuscript and photographic formats are a unique research collection for all who would wish to study and understand the emotions, nightmares, dreams, and determination of former slaves in the United States.

The slave narrative sound recordings, manuscript materials, and photographs are invaluable as windows through which we can observe and be touched by the experiences of slaves who lived in the mid-19th century. At the same time, these archival materials are the fruits of an extraordinary documentary effort of the 1930s. The federal government, as part of its response to the Great Depression, organized unprecedented national initiatives to document the lives, experiences, and cultural traditions of ordinary Americans. The slave narratives, as documents of the Federal Writers Project, established and delineated our modern concept of "oral history." Oral history, made possible by the advent of sound recording technology, was "invented" by folklorists, writers, and other cultural documentarians under the aegis of the Library of Congress and various WPA offices—especially the Federal Writers' project—during the 1930s. Oral history has subsequently become both a new tool for the discipline of history, and a new cultural pastime undertaken in homes, schools, and communities by Americans of all walks of life. The slave narratives you read in the pages that follow stand as our first national exploration of the idea of oral history, and the first time that ordinary Americans were made part of the historical record.

The American Folklife Center has expanded upon the WPA tradition by continuing to collect oral histories from ordinary Americans. Contemporary projects such as our Veterans History Project, StoryCorps Project, Voices of Civil Rights Project, as well as our work to capture the stories of Americans after September 11, 2001 and of the survivors of Hurricanes Katrina and Rita, are all adding to the Library of Congress holdings that will enrich the history books of the future. They are the oral histories of the 21st century.

Frederick Douglas once asked: can "the white and colored people of this country be blended into a common nationality, and enjoy together...under the same flag, the inestimable blessings of life, liberty, and the pursuit of happiness, as neighborly citizens of a common country? I believe they can." We hope that the words of the former slaves in these editions from Applewood Books will help Americans achieve Frederick Douglas's vision of America by enlarging our understanding of the legacy of slavery in all of our lives. At the same time, we in the American Folklife Center and the Library of Congress hope these books will help readers understand the importance of oral history in documenting American life and culture—giving a voice to all as we create our common history.

Peggy A. Bulger

Peggy Bulger
Director, The American Folklife Center
Library of Congress

A NOTE FROM THE PUBLISHER

Since 1976, Applewood Books has been republishing books from America's past. Our mission is to build a picture of America through its primary sources. The book you hold in your hand is a testament to that mission. Published in cooperation with the Library of Congress, this collection of slave narratives is reproduced exactly as writers in the Works Progress Administration's Federal Writers' Project (1936–1938) originally typed them.

As publishers, we thought about how to present these documents. Rather than making them more readable by resetting the type, we felt that there was more value in presenting the narratives in their original form. We believe that to fully understand any primary source, one must understand the period of time in which the source was written or recorded. Collected seventy years after the emancipation of American slaves, these narratives had been preserved by the Library of Congress, fortunately, as they were originally created. In 1941, the Library of Congress microfilmed the typewritten pages on which the narratives were originally recorded. In 2001, the Library of Congress digitized the microfilm and made the narratives available on their American Memory web site. From these pages we have reproduced the original documents, including both the marks of the writers of the time and the inconsistencies of the type. Some pages were missing or completely illegible, and we have used a simple typescript provided by the Library of Congress so that the page can be read. Although the font occasionally can make these narratives difficult to read, we believe that it is important not only to preserve the narratives of the slaves but also to preserve the documents themselves, thereby commemorating the groundbreaking effort that produced them. That way, also, we can give you, the reader, not only a collection of the life stories of ex-slaves, but also a glimpse into the time in which these stories were collected, the 1930s.

These are powerful stories by those who lived through slavery. No institution was more divisive in American history than slavery. From the very founding of America and to the present day, slavery has touched us all. We hope these real stories of real lives are preserved for generations of Americans to come.

INFORMANTS

INTERVIEW

FRANCES BATSON

1213 Scovel St.

Nashville, Tennessee

"I dunno jes how ole I ez. I wuz baw'n 'yer in Nashville,
durin' slabery. I must be way pas' 90 fer I member de Yankee
soldiers well. De chilluns called dem de 'blue mans.' Mah
white folks wuz named Crockett. Dr. Crockett wuz our marster
but I don't member 'im mahse'f. He d'ed w'en I wuz small. Mah
marster wuz mean ter mah mammy w'en her oler chilluns would run
'way. Mah oler br'er went ter war wid mah marster. Mah younger
br'er run 'way, dey caught 'im, tuk 'im home en whup'd 'im. He
run 'way en wuz nebber found."

"We wuzn't sold but mah mammy went 'way, en lef' me en I
got up one mawnin' went ter mah mammy's room, she wuz gon'.
I cried en cried fer her. Mah Missis wouldn't let me outa' de
house, fer fear I'd try ter find her. Atter freedum mah br'er en
a Yankee soldier kum in a waggin en git us. Mah white folks sed,
I don' see why you ez takin' dez chilluns. Mah brudder said,
'We ez free now.' I member one whup'in mah missis gib me. Me
en her daughter slipped 'way ter de river ter fish. We kotch a
fish en mah missis had hit cooked fer us but whup'd us fer goin'
ter de river."

"Whar de Buena Vista schul ez hit useter be a Yankee soldiers
Barrick. Eber mawnin' dey hadder music. We chilluns would go on
de hill, (whar the bag mill ez now) en listen ter dem. I member
a black hoss de soldiers had, dat ef you called 'im Jeff Davis
he would run you."

"I member de ole well on Cedar Street, neah de Capitol, en six mules fell in hit. Dat wuz back w'en blackberries wuz growin' on de Capitol Hill. En Morgan Park wuz called de pleasure gyarden. En hit wuz full ob Yankee soldiers. Atter de war dere wuz so many German peeple ober 'yer, dat fum Jefferson Street, ter Clay Street, wuz called Dutch town."

"I wuzn't bawn w'en de sta'rs fell. We didn't git nothin' w'en we wuz freed. Dunno much 'bout de Klu Klux Klan."

"Mah mammy useter tell me how de white folks would hire de slaves out ter mek money fer de marster en she tole me sum ob de marsters would hide dere slaves ter keep de Yankees fum gittin' dem."

"I don' b'leeve in white en black ma'iages. Mah sistah ma'ied a lite man. I wouldin' marry one ef hit would turn me ter gold. Dunno nothin' 'bout votin', allus tho't dat wuz fer de men."

"I can't think ob any tales er nuthin 'bout ghos'. 'Cept one 'bout a marster tyin' a nigger ter a fence en wuz beatin' 'im. A Yankee kum 'long made 'im untie de nigger en den de nigger beat de white man."

"Dis young peeples ez tough. I think half ob dem'll be hung, de way dey throw rocks at ole peeples. Dat's why I's crippled now, a white boy hit me wid a rock. I b'long ter de Methodist Chuch."

"Since freedum I'se hired out, washed en cooked fer diff'ent peeple. De only song I member: 'Hark Fum de Ground dis Mournful Sound.'"

INTERVIEW

JULIA CASEY

811 9th Avenue, So.

Nashville, Tennessee

I wuz bawn in West Tennessee en wuz six y'ars ole w'en war broke out.

Mah Missis wuz Miss Jennie McCullough en she ma'ried Eldridge Casey. Mah Missis's mammy wuz a widder en she gib me, mah mammy, mah sistah Violet, mah two br'ers Andrew en Alfred ter Miss Jennie fer a wed'un gif'. Missis Jennie en Marster Eldridge brung us ter Nashville 'fore de war sta'ted.

Mah Missis wuz good ter us. I'se bin w'll tuk keer ob, plenty ter eat en warm clothes ter w'ar. Right now I'se got on long underw'ar en mah chemise.

Mah mammy d'ed fust y'ar ob freedum. Dey tuk her 'way in a two-hoss waggin, 'bout four o'clock one evenin'. Dere wuz no hurses er caskets den. W'en mah mammy d'ed, I still stayed wid Missis Jennie. She raised me. Dat's why folks say I'se so peculiar. De Yankee soldiers tuk mah sistah en two br'ers 'way durin' de war. I ez de mammy ob seven chilluns. All d'ed now but one.

Mah white folks didn't send me ter schul but I'se l'arned a few things ob how ter act. Don't ax me 'bout der young peeple. Dey ez pas' me. No manners 'tall.

In slavery days you didn't hab ter worry 'bout yo clothes en rations but dese days you hab ter worry 'bout eve'ything.

I 'longs ter de Baptist Chuch. Useter go ter camp-meetin's en hab a big time wid good things ter eat. Didn't go ter de

baptizin' much. Dey would leave de chuch singin' en shoutin'.
Dere ez three days in September dat we hab dinnah on de groun'
en all Baptist git tergedder. We calls hit de 'sociation.

I'se neber voted cose dat ez de man's job. Mah frens hab
nebber had political jobs. Don't b'leeve in ma'rige ob white en
black en hit shouldn't be 'lowed.

Since freedum mah main job wuz cookin' but I'se done washin'
en ironin'. Atter mah health started failing, I done a lot ob
nusin'.

I'se aint abul ter wuk fur de las' five y'ars en de white
folks hab he'ped me. De relief gibes me groc'eys, coal en pays
mah rent. I hope ter git de ole age pension soon. Mah ole
favo'ite song ez "Mazing Grace, How Sweet hit Sounds."

INTERVIEW

CECELIA CHAPPEL

705 Allison Street

Nashville, Tenn.

"I'se bawn in Marshall County, Tennessee. I'm de olest ob ten chilluns en I'se 102 ya'rs ole. I feels lak I'se bin 'yer longer dan dat. Mah mammy wuz brought ter Nashville en sold ter sum peeple dat tuck her ter Mississippi ter live."

"Mah Marster en Missus wuz named Bob en Nancy Lord. Eve!y slave had ter say Missus en Marster en also ter de white babies. I still says hit, en ef I kum ter yo do'r, I nebber kums in 'till you ax me. Lots ob mah folks seze ter me dat I ez too ole fash'on en I seze I don' keer I wuz raised wid manners en too ole ter change."

"Our Marster gib us good food en clothes. I wuz l'arnt how ter nit, weav, sew en spin. On rainy days we wuz gib a certain 'mount ob weavin' ter do en had ter git hit don'. I dunno how ter read er rite. De white folks didn' 'low us ter l'arn nuthin'. I declar' you bettuh not git kotch wid a papah in you han'. Ef I had half a chance lak you chilluns hab, I'd go ter bed wid mah books."

"Our Marster 'lowed us ter go ter chuch. I went bar'foot en had a rag tied 'roun mah haid en mah dress kum up ter mah 'nees. Dat preacher-man would git up dere en

tell us "Now you min' yo Marster en Missis en don' steal
fum dem;" I stayed wid mah Missis fer a long time atter
I got freedum en I cried lak a fool w'en I had ter leave
dem. Mah Missis seze "You ez jes as free as I ez," but I
allus had good clothes en good food en I didn' know how
I'd git dem atter I lef' her."

"Mah white folks wuz tight on us but, as ole as I ez,
I offun think dat dey nebber hit a lick dat I didn' need.
Ef'n dey hadn' raised me right, I might hab got in meaness
en bin locked up half de time, but I ain't nebber bin 'rested, en I'se 'ferd ob de policemans. De fiel' slaves wuz
whup'd in de fiel's by de oberseer en de Marster en Missis
did hit at de house."

"I tell you we had a hahd time. Mah Missis woulden'
let dem sell me. I wuz a nuss en house gal. I wuz whup'd
wid a bull whup, en got cuts on mah back menny a time. I'se
not shamed ter say I got skyars on mah back now fum Marster
cuttin' hit wid dat bull whup. Mah Missis also whup'd me.
W'en de Missis got ready ter whup me, she would gib us sum
wuk ter do, so she would kind ob git ober her mad spell 'fore
she whup'd us. Sum times she would lock us up in a dark
closet en bring our food ter us. I hated bein' locked up.
Atter dey tuk me out ob de house, I wuked in de fiel' lak
de urthurs. Long 'fore day break, we wuz standin' in de
fiel's leanin' on our hoes waitin' fer daylite en waitin'
fer de horn ter blow so we would start ter wuk. Ef'n we

wan'ed ter go ter any place we had ter hab a pass wid our
Marster's name on hit en ef you didn' hab hit, you got tore
ter pieces en den you Marster tore you up w'en you got home. "

"One story mah daddy useter tell us wuz 'bout a slave
named Pommpy. He wuz allus prayin' fer de good Lawd ter tek
'im 'way. One nite he wuz down on his 'nees prayin', "Good
Lawd, kum en tek po Pommpy out ob his misery." De Marster
ob Pommpy 'year'd 'm en de Marster made a leetle noise en
Pommpy seze, "Who ez dat?" En his Marster seze, "Hits de
Lawd kum ter tek po Pommpy out ob his misery." Pommpy crawl
under de bed en seze, "Pommpy has bin gon' two er three days."

"'Nurther story: A partridge en a fox 'greed ter kil'
a beef. Dey kilt en skinned hit. B'fo dey divide hit de fox
said, "Mah wife seze sen' her sum beef fer soup," so he tuck
a piece ob hit en carried hit down de hill, den kum back en
said mah wife wants mo' beef fer soup. He kep dis up 'til
all de beef wuz gon' 'cept de libber. De fox kum back en
de partridge seze now lets cook dis libber en both ob us
eat hit. De partridge cooked de libber, et hits part rite
quick, en den fell ovuh lak hit wuz sick; de fox got skeered
en said dat beef ez pizen en he ran down de hill en started
bringin' de beef back en w'en he brought hit all back, he lef'
en de partridge had all de beef."

"Don't member much now 'bout de Klu Klux Klan en
nothin' 'bout slave 'risings at any place. I don' member
'bout de sta'rs fallin', but I did see de comet, en hit

looked lak a sta'r wid a long tail; atter freedum, I nebber
year'd ob no slave gettin' land er money en I dunno nothin'
'bout de slave mart 'yer fer I didn' git ter kum ter town."

"Since freed, I hab nussed, cooked en don' diff'unt
things. I wuk'ed fer one family fifteen y'ars en didn' miss
a day. I has stayed at dis place fer de las' five y'ars.
I had a stroke en wuz in de hospit'l a long time. I cain' git
out; en 'roun' 'yer in de house, I has ter walk wid a stick."

"I ain' nebber voted. One day sum men kum 'yer ter
tek me ter vote. I tole dem w'en I got ready ter be a man,
I would put on overalls."

"I'se a member ob de Missionary Baptist Chuch. I
ain' bin fer a long time kaze I ain' able ter go. De ole
song I members ez "Dixie Land," en "Run Nigger Run, de Pat-
a rollers Will Git You."

"Oh Lawdy! I think sum ob is young peeple ain' no
count w'ile sum ob dem ez alright. I think each color should
ma'rie his own color. Hit makes me mad ter think 'bout hit.
Ef de good Lawd had wanted dat, he would hab had us all one
color."

"Fer a long time de relief gib me a quart ob milk a
day, but now all I has ez w'at mah sistah Harriett gibs me.
She sin' got much wuk en sum days we don' hab much ter eat.
Ef mah Missis wuz livin' I wouldin' go hongry."

410072

INTERVIEW

WILEY CHILDRESS

808 Gay St.

Nashville, Tennessee

"I'se 83 Y'ars ole en wuz bawn a slave. Mah mammy b'longed ter de Bosley's en mah daddy b'longed ter de Scales.

"W'en Miss Jane Boxley ma'ried Marster Jerry Scales, me en mah mammy, br'er en sistah wuz gib ter Miss Jane."

"Durin' de war mah Missis tuk mah mammy en us chilluns wid her ter de mount'ins 'till de war wuz gon'. Did'nt see no soldiers. Don't member now nuthin' 'bout dem Klu Klux men en don't member de ole songs er 'bout slaves votin'."

"Dunno 'bout de young persons, white er black, dey ez all so wild now."

"W'en we all wuz freed we had nuthin en no place ter go, so dat mah mammy lived wid out Missis five y'ars longer."

"De only story dat I member mah people tole me 'bout wuz on Fedd, a slave on de next plantation. He wuz a big man en wuz de strongest man neah dat part ob de kuntry. He wouldin' 'low nobody ter whup 'in. De Marster framed 'im by tellin' 'im ter bring his saddle hoss en w'en he kum wid de hoss several men 'peahrd en tole Fedd dat dey wuz gonna whup 'im. He struck one ob de mans so hahd dey had ter hab de doctuh. De Marster said let 'im 'lone he's too strong ter be whup'd. I'll hab ter shoot 'im. One time Fedd run 'way en de white men whar he stopped know'd he wuz a good fighter en made a $250.00 bet dat nobody could lick 'im. A nigger fum de iron wuks fought Fedd en Fedd won. De iron wuks nigger wuz kilt right dere.

"'fore Freedum de slaves wuz promused forty acres ob land w'en freed but none eber got hit, en I 'year'd ob no one gittin' any money. I dunno nuthin' ob de slave 'risin's, ghostus er dreams, but I member mah folks talkin' 'bout fallin' sta'rs en a comet but I don' member now w'at dey said."

"I'se wuk'd at a lot ob diff'ent jobs since mah freedum. I wuk'd at de Maxwell House 15 years as store room porter, en hit wuz de only wo'th-while hotel in Nashville at dat time. I wuk'd fuh de City fuh menny y'ars en den I wuk'd fuh Foster & Creighton 'till dey wore me out. I off'n think ob deze diff'nt men dat I wuk'd fuh but dey ez all de'd. De las' job I had wuz buildin' fiers en odd jobs fuh a lady up de street. She would gib me food en coal. She ez de'd now."

"I'se not able ter wuk now en all I has ez a small groc'ey order dat de relief gibs me. Dey keep promisin' ter gib me de Old Age Pension en I wish dey would hurry hit up."

410025

SUBJECT

SLAVE STORIES

ROBERT FALLS
608 South Broadway
Knoxville, Tennessee

Interviewed by

Della Yoe, Foreman
Federal Writers' Project,
First District, WPA
Room # 215 Old YMCA Building
State and Commerce Streets.
Knoxville, Tennessee

Robert Falls was born on December I4,I840,in the rambling one-story
shack that accomodated the fifteen slaves of his Old Marster,Beattie Goforth,on
a farm in Claiborne County,North Carolina.   His tall frame is slightly stooped,
but he is not subjected to the customary infirmities of the aged, other than
poor vision and hearing. Fairly comfortable , he is spending his declining years
in contentment, for he is now the first consideration of his daughter,Mrs.Lola
Reed, with whom he lives at #608 S.Broadway,Knoxville,Tennessee. His cushioned
rocking chair is the honor seat of the household.His apology for not offering it
to visitors, is that he is " not so fast on his feet as he used to be."

Despite Uncle Robert's protest that his " mind comes and goes", his
memory is keen,and his sense of humor unimpaired. His reminiscences of slave days
are enriched by his ability to recreate scenes and incidents in few words, and by
his powers of mimicry. "If I had my life to live over," he declares," I would die
fighting rather than be a slave again. I want no man's yoke on my shoulders no
more. But in them days, us niggers didnt know no better, All we knowed was work,
and hard work. We was learned to say,'Yes Sir!' and scrape down and bow, and to
do just exactly what we was told to do, make no difference if we wanted to or not.
Old Marster and Old Mistress would say,"Do this!" and we don it. And they say,
' Come here!' and if we didnt come to them,they come to us. And they brought the
bunch of switches with them."

" They didnt half feed us either. They fed the animals better.They
gives the mules, ruffage and such, to chaw on all night.But they didnt give us
nothing to chaw on. Learned us to steal, that's what they done.Whay we would
take anything we could lay our hands on,when we was hungry.Then they'd whip us
for lieing when we say we dont know nothing about it. But it was easier to stand,
when the stomach was full."

" Now my father, he was a fighter. He was mean as a bear. He was so bad to fight and so troublesome he was sold four times to my knowing and maybe a heap more times. That's how come my name is Falls, even if some does call me Robert Goforth. Niggers would change to the name of their new marster, every time they was sold. And my father had a lot of names, but kep the one of his marster when he got a good home. That man was Harry Falls. He said he'd been trying to buy father for a long time, because he was the best waggoner in all that country abouts. And the man what sold him to Falls, his name was Collins, he told my father," You so mean, I got to sell you. You all time complaining about you dont like your white folks. Tell me now who you wants to live with. Just pick your man and I will go see him." Then my father tells Collins, I want you to sell me to Marster Harry Falls. They made the trade. I disremember what the money was, but it was big. Good workers sold for $1,000 and $2,000. After that the white folks didnt have no more trouble with my father. But he'd still fight. That man would fight a she-bear and lick her every time."

" My mother was sold three times before I was born. The last time when Old Goforth sold her, to the slave speculators,-you know every time they needed money they would sell a slave,- and they was taking them, driving them, just like a pack of mules, to the market from North Carolina into South Carolina, she begun to have fits. You see they had sold her away from her baby. And just like I tell you she begun having fits. They got to the jail house where they was to stay that night, and she took on so, Jim Slade and Press Worthy- them was the slave speculators, couldnt do nothing with her. Next morning one of them took her back to Marse Goforth and told him, "Look here. We cant do nothing with this woman. You got to take her and give us back our money. And do it now," they says. And they mean it too. So Old Marse Goforth took my mother and give them back their money. After that none of us was ever separated. We all lived, a brother and two sisters and my mother, with the Goforths till free-dom."

" And do you know, she never did get over having fits. She had them
every change of the moon, or leastways every other moon change. But she kept
on working.She was a hard worker.She had to be.Old Mistress see to that.She
was meaner than old Marster, she was. She would sit by the spinning wheel
and count the turns the slave women made.And they couldnt fool her none neither.
My mother worked until ten o'clock almost every night because her part was to
'spend so many cuts" a day, and she couldnt get through no sooner. "hen I was
a little shaver, I used to sit on the floor with the other little fellows while
our mothers worked, and sometimes the white folks girls would read us a Bible
story.But most of the time we slept.Right there on the floor.   Then later,when
I was bigger, I had to work with the men at night shelling corn, to take to
town early mornings."

        "Marster Goforth counted himself a good old Baptist christian. The
one good deed he did, I will never forget, he made us all go to church every
Sunday. That was the onliest place off the farm we ever went. Every time a slave
went off the place, he had to have a pass, except we didnt, for church. Everybody in thet country knowed that the Goforth niggers didnt have to have no pass
to go to church. But that didnt make no difference to the Pattyroolers. They'd
hide in the bushes, or wait along side of the road, and when the niggers come
from meeting, the Pattyroolers's say,'Whar's your pass'? Us Goforth niggers used
to start running soon as we was out of church.We never got caught.That is why I
tell you I cant use my legs like I used to. If you was caught without no pass,
the Pattyroolers give you five licks.They was licks! You take a bunch of five to
seven Pattyroolers each giving five licks and the blood flows."

        "Old Marster was too old to go to the war.He had one son was a soldier,
but he never come home again. I never seen a soldier till the war was over and
they begin to come back to the farms. We half-grown niggers had to work the farm,
because all the farmers had to give,-I believe it was a tenth- of their crops to

help feed the soldiers. So we didnt know nothing about what was going on, no more than a hog. It was a long time before we knowed we was free. Then one night Old Marster come to our house and he say he wants to see us all before breakfast tomorrow morning and to come on over to his house.He got something to tell us."

"Next morning we went over there. I was the monkey, always acting smart.But I believe they liked me better than all of the others. I just spoke sassy-like and say,"Old Marster, what you got to tell us"? My mother said, "Shut your mouth fool.He'll whip you!" And Old Marster say,-"No I wont whip you.Never no more. sit down thar all of you and listen to what I got to tell you.I hates to do it but I must. You all aint my Niggers no more. You is free. Just as free as I am.Here I have raised you all to work for me, and now you are going to leave me. I am an old man, and I cant get along without you.I dont know what I am going to do." Well sir, it killed him.He was dead in less than ten months."

" Everybody left right now, but me and my brother and another fellow. Old Marster fooled us to believe we was duty-bound to stay with him till we was all twenty-one. But my brother, that boy was suborn. Soon he say he aint going to stay there.And he left. In about a year, maybe less, he come back and he told me I didnt have to work for Old Goforth, I was free, sure enouhh free,and I went with him and he got me a job railroading. But the work was too hard for me.I couldnt stand it.So I left there and went to my mother. I had to walk.It was forty-five miles. I made it in a day. She got me work there where she worked."

" I remember so well, how the roads was full of folks walking and walking along when the Niggers were freed. Didnt know where they was going.Just going to see about something else somewhere else. Meet a body in the road and they ask,'Where you going'?.'Dont know.'. 'What you going to do'? 'Dont know.'

And then sometimes we would meet a white man and he would say," How you like
to come work on my farm'? And we say," I dont know.' And then maybe he say,
" If you come work for me on my farm, when the crops is in I give you five
bushels of corn, five gallons of molasses, some ham-meat, and all your clothes
and vittals whils you works for me." Alright! That's what I do. And then something begins to work up here,(touching his forehead with his fingers) I begins
to think and to know things. And I knowed then I could make a living for my
own self, and I never had to be a slave no more."

        " Now, Old Marster Goforth, had four sisters what owned slaves,
and they wasnt mean to them like our Old Marster and Mistress.Some of the
old slaves and teir folks are   still living on their places right to this day.
But they never dispute none with their brother about how mean he treat his
slaves. And him claiming to be such a Christian! Well, I reckon he's found
out something about slave driving by now. The good Lord has to get his work in
some time. And he'll take care of them low down Pattyroolers and slave speculators and means Marsters and Mistress's/ He's took good care of me in the
years since I was free'd, only now, we needs Him again now and then. I just stand
up on my two feet, raise my arms to heaven, and say,"Lord,help me!' He never
fails me.I asked him this morning,didnt I Lola ? Asked him to render help.We
need it. And here you come. Lola, just watch that lady write. If you and me had
her education, we'd be fixed now wouldnt we? I never had no learning."

        "Thank you Lady"(tucking the coin into his pocket wallet,along
with his tobacco)And thank you for coming. It does me a heap of good to see
visitors and talk about the old times.Come again, wont you? And next time you
come, I want to talk to you about old age pensions. I come here from Marian,N.C.
three years ago, and they tell me I have to live here four, before I gets a pension. And as I dont left North Carolina, I cant get a pension from them.But
maybe you can tell me what to do. I likes this place.And I do hopes I get a
pension before I gets to be a hundred."

INTERVIEW

RACHEL GAINES

1025 10th Ave. N.

Nashville, Tennessee

"Lawdy! I'se dunno how ole I ez. B'leeves I'se 'round 95 ter 100 y'ars. De fust thing I members ez I wuz tuk in a waggin ter Trenton, Kentucky en sold ter Dr. Bainbridge Dickerson jest lak dey sold cows en hosses. Mah sistah wuz sold in de same way at Bowling Green, Kentucky ter 'nuther Marster."

"I wuz sold only one time in mah life en dat wuz w'en Marster Dickinson bought me. Atter freedum wuz 'clared de Marster tole all his slaves dat dey could go wharever'y dey pleased but ef'n dey couldn't mek dere own livin' ter kum ter 'im en he would he'ps dem."

"Missus Dickinson kep' me dere kaze I wuz nuss ter dere son Howard who wuz sho a wild one. I member how he would tote out fried chicken, pig meat en uthuh good stuff ter us darkies. Dey 'greed ter pay me $35.00 a yeah (en keep) en hit wuz gib me eve'y Christmus mawning. Dey treated me good, gib me all de clothes en uthuh things I needed ez ef'n I wuz one ob de fam'ly."

"Eve'y two weeks de Marster would sen' fer Jordan McGowan who wuz de leader ob a string music ban'. Dey would git dere Friday nite early en de slaves would dance in de grape house dat nite en all day Saturday up ter midnite. You don't hab now as good dance music en as much fun as de ole time days had. We allus had a big barbecue er watermelon feast eve'y time we

had a dance. Neber 'gin 'll dere be as good times as we
useter hab. In mah time we neber y'ard ob wukouses er pen
but now dey ez all filled.

"I kin see now in mah mind de ole ice house on de plantation. In de wint'r de slaves would fill hit wid ice dey got
off de crik en hit wuz not used 'til warm wedder cum. 'nother
thing I members ez de "Pat-a-rollers" (she refers to the Police
Patrol of that day) who would kotch en whup runaway slaves en
slaves 'way fum dere own plantations widout a pass wid dere
Marsters name signed on hit."

"I member w'en Nashville fust had street cars pulled
'long by hosses er mules en I also member de ole dummy cars,
run by steam, ter Glendale Park also New Town (now called West
Nashville)."

"We had sum bad en good luck signs but I'se fergettin' sum,
but I'se members 'bout a black cat crossin' ovuh de path in
frunt ob you dat you sho would hab bad luck. W'en dat happened
ter me, I would spit on de ground, turn 'round en back ober de
place de cat crossed en de "bad luck" wuz gon' fum me. Ef'n you
found a ole hoss shoe dat had bin drapt'd by de hoss, hit meant
good luck. Sum peeples, white en black, w'en dey fin' a hoss
shoe, dey would tack hit up on de frunt door frame wid de toe
ter de groun'.

"Atter de Marster en Missus d'ed, I went ter Nashville en
made mah way fur menny y'ars by washin' en ironin' fer white
peeple but atter I went blind I kum 'yer ter live wid mah
daughter."

INTERVIEW

FRANKIE GOOLE

204 5th Ave. So.

Nashville, Tenn.

"I wuz bawn in Smith County on uther side ob Lebanon. Ah'll
be 85 y'ars ole Christmas Day.

Mah ole Missis wuz named Sallie, en mah Marster wuz George
Waters. Mah mammy's name wuz Lucindia, she wuz sold fum me w'en
I wuz six weeks ole, en mah Missis raised me. I allus slept wid
her. Mah Missis wuz good ter me, but (her son) mah Marster whup'd
me.

Dunno ob any ex-slaves votin' er holdin' office ob any kin.

I member de Ku Klux Klan en Pat-a-rollers. Dey would kum
'roun en whup de niggers wid a bull whup. Ef'n dey met a niggah
on de road dey'd say, "Whar ez you gwin dis time ob mawnin'?"
De slaves would say, "We ez gwine ovuh 'yer ter stay aw'ile,"
en den dey would start beatin' dem. I'se stood in our do'er en
'yeard de hahd licks, en screams ob de ones dat wuz bein' whup'd,
en I'd tell mah Missis, "Listen ter dat." She would say, "See,
dat ez w'at will happen ter you ef'n you try ter leave." I
member one nite a Ku Klux Klan rode up ter our do'er. I tole
mah Missis sum body wuz at de do'er wantin' ter know whar mah
Marster wuz. She tole 'im he wuz d'ed en her son had gon' 'way
dat mawnin'. He hunted all thro de house, en up in de loft, en
said whar ez de niggers? Mah Missis tole i'm dey wuz down in de
lettle house. He went down dere, woke dem up, axed dem 'bout
dere Marster en den whup'd all ob dem. Ef dey had de Ku Klux Klan
now dere wouldin' be so manny peeples on de kounty road en in

de pen.

I useter drive up de cows en mah feet would be so cole en mah toes cracked open en bleedin', en I'd be cryin' 'til I got almos' ter de house den I'd wipe mah eyes on de bottom ob mah dress, so de Marster wouldn' know dat I had bin cryin'. He'd say, "Frankie ain't you cryin'?" I'd say, "No suh." "Ez you cole?" "Yes, sir." He would say kum on en warm.

W'en de niggers wuz freed, all ob mah Missis slaves slipped 'way, 'cept me. One mawnin' she tole me ter go down en wake dem up, I went down en knocked, no body said nuthin'. I pushed on de do'er - hit kum op'n - en I fell in de room en hurt mah chin. I went back ter Missis - en she sezs, "W'at ez de matter wid you?" I sezs, "Uncle John en all ob dem ez gon'; I pushed on de do'er en fell in." She sezs you know dey ez not gone, go back en git dem up. I had ter go back, but dey wur'ent dere.

No, I don't member de sta'rs fallin'.

Mah Missis didunt gib me nuthin, cept mah clothes, en she put dem in a carpet bag. Atter freedum mah mammy kum fum Lebanon en got me. Ah'll neber fergit dat day - Oh Lawdy! I kin see her now. Mah ole Missis' daughter-in-law had got a bunch ob switches ter whup me, I wuz standin' in de do'er shakin' all ovuh, en de young Missis wuz tellin' me ter git mah clothes off. I sezs, "I se'd a 'oman kum'g thro de gate." Mah Missis sezs, "Dat ez Lucindia" en de young Missis hid de switches. Mah mammy sezs I'se kum ter git mah chile. Mah Missis tole her ter let me spend de nite wid her, den she'd send me ter de Court House at 9 o'clock next mawnin'. So I stayed wid de Missis dat nite, en she tole me ter alluz be a good girl, en don't let a man er boy trip me. I didunt know w'at she mean but I allus membered w'at

she said. I guess I wuz 'bout 12 y'ars ole w'en I lef' mah
Missis en mah mammy brought me ter Nashville en put me ter
wuk. De mawnin' I lef' mah Missis, I went ter de Court House
en met mah mammy; de Court room wuz jammed wid peeple. De
Jedge tole me ter hold my right hand up, I wuz so skeered I
stuck both hands up. Jedge sezs, "Frankie ez dat yo mammy?"
I sezs, "I dunno, she sezs she ez." (W'at did I know ob a
mammy dat wuz tuk fum me at six weeks ole). He sezs, "Wuz yo
Marster good ter you?" I sezs, "Mah Missis wuz, but mah Marster
wasn't - he whup'd me." De Jedge said, "Whar did he whup you?"
I tole him on mah back. He sezs, "Frankie, ez you laughin'?"
I sezs, "No, sir." He said ter mah mammy, "Lucindia tek dis
chile en be good ter her fer she has b'en mistreated. Sum day
she can mek a livin' fer you." (En thank de Lawd I did keep
her in her ole days en wuz able ter bury her.) At dat time
money wuz called chin plaster en w'en I lef' out ob de court
room diff'ent peeple gib me money en I had mah hat almos' full.
Dat wuz de only money I had gib ter me.

I nussed Miss Sadie Pope Fall; she ma'ried Mat Gardner. I
also nussed Miss Sue Porter Houston. I den wuk'd at de Bline
Schul.

De fust pa'r ob shoes I eber had wuz atter I kum ter
Nashville. Dey had high tops en wuz called bootees. I had sum
red striped socks wid dem.

De ole songs I member:

"De Ole Time 'ligion."
"I'm Goin' ter Join de Ban."

W'en dey would sing deze songs hit would almos' mek you ha'r
stand up on yo haid, de way dem peeples would jump en shout!

I member w'en sum ob de slaves run 'way durin' slavery.

I dunno any tales; mah mammy wasn't a 'oman ter talk much. Maybe ef she had bin I would hab had an easier time. As far as I know de ex-slaves hab had diff'ent kinds ob wuk since dere freedum. No, I ain' nebber se'd any ghos'. I'se bin in de woods en dark places, but didn't see nothin', en I'se not goin' ter say I did kaze I might git par'lized.

I went ter schul one y'ar at Fisk in de y'ar 1869.

De last man I wuk'd fer wuz at de Link Hotel. Den I started keepin' boarders. Hab fed all deze Nashville police. De police ez de ones dat hep'ed git deze relief orders fer me. I hab lived on dis street fer 60 years. I lived 22 y'ars whar de Hermitage Laundry ez. Dat ez whar I got de name "Mammie." W'iles livin' dere I raised eighteen chilluns white en black, en sum ob dem iz good ter me now.

I had sum papah's 'bout mah age en diff'ent things, but w'en de back waters got up, dey got lost. I didn't hab ter move but I kep prayin' en talkin' ter de Lawd en I b'leeve he 'Yeard me fer de water didn't git in mah house.

I member w'en de yellow fever en de cholera wuz 'yer, in 1870 en 1873. Dey didn't hab coffins nuff ter put dem in, so dey used boxes en piled de boxes in waggins lak hauling wood.

I'se aint worth a dime now w'en hit kums ter wukin' fer I'se aint able ter do nuthin, thoo I can't complain ob mah livin' since de relief has bin takin' keer ob me.

Dis young peeples, "Oh mah Lawd!" Dey ain' worth talkin' 'bout. I tries ter shame deze 'omen, dey drink (I call hit ole bust haid whiskey), en do such mean things. I'se disgusted at mah own color. Dey try ter know ter much, en dunno muthin', en dey don' do 'nuff wuk.

I nebber voted en dunno nothin' 'bout hit. Hab nebber had any frens in office. Cain' member nothin' 'bout re'structon. I hab bin sick en still don' feel right. Sumtimes I feels krazy.

Hab bin tole dat black cat crossin' road in frunt ob you wuz bad luck. I nebber did b'leeve in any signs. Ef I ez ter hab bad luck, ah'll hab hit.

I b'long ter de Baptist Chuch.

De culored peeples useter hab camp meetin's, en dey'd last fer two weeks. Lawd hab mercy did we hab a time at dem meetin's, preachin', singin', en shoutin'. En ovuh sum whar neah dey would be cookin' mutton en diff'ent good things ter eat. Sum ob dem would shout 'til dere throats would be sore en hit seemed dat sum ob dem niggahs didn't keer ef dey got home ter wuk er not.

I sumtimes wish fer de good ole days. Deze days folks don't hab time fer 'ligion. De dog-gone ole radio en udder things ez takin' hits place.

Oh Lawdie how dey did baptize down at de wha'f. De Baptist peeple would gather at de wha'f on de fust Sunday in May. Dey would kum fum all de Baptist Chuches. Would leave de chuch singin' en shoutin' en keep dat up 'til dey got ter de river. Hab seen dem wid new clothes on git down on de groun en roll en git covered wid dirt. Sum ob dem would almos' luze dere clothes, en dey'd fall down lak dey wuz dying.

Deze last few y'ars dey hab got ter stylish ter shout.

INTERVIEW

Precilla Gray

807 Ewing Ave.

Nashville, Tenn.

I think I'se 107 Y'ars olè. Wuz bawn in Williamson County 'fore
de Civil wah. Guess de reason I hab libed so long wuz cose I tuk good
keer ob mahself en wore warm clo'es en still do, w'ar mah yarn petty-
coats now. Hab had good health all mah life. Hab tuk very lettle
medicine en de wust sickness I eber had wuz small-pox. I'se bin a
widah 'bout 70 y'ars.

Mah mammy d'ed w'en I wuz young but mah daddy libed ter be 103
y'ars ole. I nebber went ter schul a day in mah life, ma'ied 'fore
freedum en w'en I got free, had ter wuk all de time ter mek a libin'
fer mah two chillen. One libes in California en I lives wid de uther,
tergedder wid mah great, great, grandson, five y'ars ole, in Nashville.

Mah fust marster en missis wuz Amos en Sophia Holland en he made
a will dat we slaves wuz all ter be kep' among de fam'ly en I wuz heired
fum one fam'ly ter 'nother. Wuz owned under de "will" by Haddas Holland,
Missis Mary Haddock en den Missis Synthia Ma'ied Sam Pointer en I libed
wid her 'til freedum wuz 'clared.

Mah fust mistress had three looms en we had ter mek clothes fer
ev'ery one on de plan'ashun. I wuz taught ter weav', card, spin en
'nit en ter wuk in de fiel's. I wuz 'feared ob de terbacker wums at
fust but Aunt Frankie went 'long by me en showed me how ter pull de
wum's head off. Hab housed terbacker till 9 o'clock at nite. Our
marster whupped us w'en we needed hit. I got memny a whuppin'.

Marster Amos wuz a great hunter en had lots ob dogs en me en
mah cousin had de job ob cookin' dog food en feedin' de dogs. One
day de marster went huntin' en lef' three dogs in de pen fer us ter

feed. One ob de dogs licked out ob de pan en we got a bunch ob switches
en started wearin' de dogs out. We thought de marster wuz miles 'way
w'en he walked up on us. He finished wearin' de bunch ob swithhes out
on us. Dat wuz a whuppin' I'll nebber fergit.

W'en I wuz heired ter Missis Synthis, I wuked in de fiel's 'til
she started ter raise chillens en den I wuz kep in de house ter see
atter dem. Missis had a lot ob cradles en dey kep two 'omen in dat
room takin' keer ob de babies en lettle chillens 'longin' ter dere
slaves. Soon as de chillens, wuz seven y'ars ole. dey started dem
ter 'nittin'.

Marster Sam Pointer, husband of Missis Synthis, wus a good man
en he wuz good ter us en he fed en clothed us good. We wore yarn hoods,
sha'ls, en pantletts which wuz 'nit things dat kum fum yo shoe tops
ter 'bove yo knees.

De marster wuz also a 'ligious man en he let us go ter chuch.
He willed land fer a culled chuch at Thompson Station. I 'longs
ter de foot washin' Baptist, called de Free Will Baptist. De marster
bought mah husband William Gray en I ma'ied 'im dere.

W'en de Civil wah wuz startin' dere wuz soldiers en tents eve'-
ywhar. I had ter 'nit socks en he'ps mek soldiers coats en durin' de
wah, de marster sent 100 ob us down in Georgia ter keep de Yankees
fum gittin' us en we camped out durin' de whole three y'ars.

I member de Klu Klux. One nite a bunch ob us went out, dey got
atter us. We waded a big crik en hid in de bushes ter keep dem fum
gittin' us.

Hab gon' ter lots ob camp-meetin's. Dey'd hab lots ob good things
ter eat en fed eberbody. Dey'd hab big baptizin's down at de Cumberland Riber, and menny things.

W'en freed, our white folks didn't gib us nuthin'. We got 'way
en hired out fer anthin' we could git. Nebber knowed ob any plantashuns

en wuz not ole er'nuff ter member de sta'rs fallin'. Songs we use'ter
sing wuz, "On Jordan's Bank I Stand en Cast a Wistful Eye en Lak Drops
ob Sweat, Lak Blood Run Down, I Shed mah Tears."

I try not ter think 'bout de ole times. Hit's bin so long ago
so I don' member any tales now.

I'se had a lot ob good times in mah day. Our white folks would
let us hab "bran dances" en we'd hab a big time. I has nebber voted
en I think dat ez a man's wuk. Don't b'leeve in signs, I hab allus
tho't whut ez gwine ter be will be, en de only way ter be ez de rite
way.

Eber since slavery I'se cooked fer peeple. I cooked fer Mr. Lea
Dillon fifteen y'ars. Wuked at de Union Depot fer y'ars. Five y'ars
fer Dr. Douglas at his Infirmary en I cooked fer en raised Mrs Grady's
baby. Hab wuked fer diff'ent folks ovuh town ter mek mah livin'. I
ain't bin able ter wuk fer eight y'ars. Dunno how much I weigh now,
I hab lost so much.(she weighs now at least 250 pounds). All de ex-
slaves I know hab wuked at diff'ent jobs lak I has.

INTERVIEW

EX-SLAVES

JENNY GREER

706 Overton, Street.

Nashville, Tennessee

"Am 84 y'ars ole en wuz bawn in Florence, Alabama, 'bout seben miles fum town. Wuz bawn on de Collier plantashun en Marster en Missis wuz James en Jeanette Collier. Mah daddy en mammy wuz named Nelson en Jane Collier. I wuz named atter one ob mah Missis' daughters. Our family wuz neber sold er divided."

"I'se bin ma'ied once. Ma'ied Neeley Greer. Thank de Lawd I aint got no chilluns. Chilluns ez so bad now I can't stand dem ter save mah life."

"Useter go ter de bap'isin's en dey would start shoutin' en singin' w'en we lef' de chuch. Went ter deze bap'isin's in Alabama, Memphis, en 'yer in Nashville. Lawdy hab mercy, how we useter sing. Only song I members ez 'De Ole Time 'ligion.' I useter go ter camp meetin's. Eve'rbody had a jolly time, preachin', shoutin' en eatin' good things."

"We didn't git a thing w'en we wuz freed. W'en dey said we wuz free mah peeple had ter look out fer demselves."

"Don' member now 'bout K.K.K. er 'structshun days. Mah mammy useter tell us a lot ob stories but I'se fergot dem. I'se neber voted en dunno ob any frens bein' in office."

"No mam, no mam, don't b'leeve in diff'ent colurs ma'rin. I member one ole sign - 'bad luck ter empty ashes atter dark.'"

"I'se hired out wuk'n in white folks house since freedum. I'se a widow now en live 'yer wid mah neice en mah sistah.

INTERVIEW

EMMA GRISHAM

1118 Jefferson St.

Nashville, Tennessee

"I wuz bawn in Nashville. I'se up in 90 y'ars, but
I tell dem I'se still young. I lived on Gallatin Pike
long 'fore de war, en uster se'd de soldiers ride by."

"Mah marsters name wuz Wm. Penn Harding. Mah daddy
wuz sold at Sparta, Tennessee 'fore I wuz bawn en Marster
Harding bought 'im. Mah mammy erready 'longed ter de
Hardings."

"I don' member much 'bout slavery I wuz small, but I
know I wore a leetle ole slip wid two er three bottons in
frunt. Mammy would wash me en I'd go out frunt en play
wid de white chilluns."

"W'en de fightin' got so heavy mah white peeple got
sum Irish peeple ter live on de plantation, en dey went
south, leavin' us wid de Irish peeple."

"I wuz leetle en I guess I didn't think much 'bout
freedum, I'd allus had plenty ter eat en w'ar."

"Dunno ob any slaves gittin' nuthin at freedum."

"Our white folks didn't whup mah peeple; but de oberseers whup'd de slaves on uther plantations."

"De Yankees had camps on de Capitol hill. En dere wuz
soldier camps in east Nashville en you had ter hab a pass
ter git thro?"

"I member w'en de pen wuz on 15th en Chuch, en de
convicts wuk'd 'round de Capitol."

"I went ter schul at Fisk a short time, w'en hit wuz
neah 12th en Cedar, en a w'ile down on Chuch St. Mah teacher
allus bragged on me fer bein' clean en neat. I didn't git
much schuling, mah daddy wuz lak mos' ole folks, he though
ef'n you knowd yo a, b, c's en could read a line, dat wuz 'nuff.
En he hired me out. Dunno w'at dey paid me, fer hit wuz paid
ter mah daddy.

"I wuz hired ter a Mrs. Ryne fer y'ars, whar de Loveman
store ez now. Dere wuz a theatre whar Montgomery Ward store
ez, a lot ob de theatre peeple roomed en bo'ded wid Mrs. Ryne,
en dey would gib me passes ter de sho' en I'd slip up in de
gall'ry en watch de sho'. I couldn't read a wud but I 'joy'd
goin'. Mah daddy wuz a driver fer Mr. Ryan.

"I nussed fer a Mrs. Mitchell en she had a boy in schul.
One summer she went 'way. A Mrs. Smith wid 10 boys wanted me
ter stay wid her 'til Mrs. Mitchell got back en I staid en laked
dem so well dat I wouldin go back ter Mrs. Mitchell's.

"I went ter Memphis en ma'ied George Grisham in 1870. He
jinned de army, as ban' leader, went ter San Antonio, Texas en
I kum back ter Mrs. Smith's en stayed 'til her mammy lost her
mind. Mah husband d'ed in Texas, fum heart truble. All his
things wuz sent back ter me, en eve'y month I got a $30.00
pension fer me en mah daughter. W'en she wuz 16 dey cut hit
down en I only git $12.00 now.

I edj'cated mah daughter at Fisk; en she's bin teachin'
schul since 1893. She buy dis place en we live tergedder.
We hab good health en both ez happy. I hab a 'oman kum eve'y
Monday en wash fer us.

"De ole songs I member ez:

     "Harp fum de Tomb dis Mournful Sound."
     "Am I a Soldier ob de Cross."

"Ole signs ez: Dream ob snakes, sign ob de'th. - Ef a
hen crows a sign ob de'th. - Sneeze wid food in mouth means
de'th. - Ef a black cat crosses de road, walk backwards 'til
you git pas' whar hit crossed. Mah parents useter tell lots
ob tales but I can't think ob dem."

"Oh honey, I dunno w'at dis young peeples ez kum'n ter. Dey
ez so diff'ent fum de way I wuz raised. I don't think much ob
dis white en black mar'ages. Hit shouldn't be 'lowed.

"I 'long ter de Missionary Baptist."

INTERVIEW

MEASY HUDSON

1209 Jefferson St.

Nashville, Tennessee

"Wuz bawn' in North Carolina en I'se 90 y'ars ole
in November. W'en war broke out we kum ter Tennessee en
hab bin 'yer eber since. Wuz 'yer w'en old Hood fi'rd
de cannons. He said he wuz kum'n 'yer ter Christmas
dinnah, but he didn't do hit."

"Mah white folks wuz named Harshaw. Marster Aaron Harshaw d'ed en we wuz willed ter his chilluns en dat we wuz
not ter be whup'd er 'bused in anyway. We wuz sold, but
long 'fore de war mah daddy wuz freed en mah manny wuz not
freed, but kep' a slave."

"De marster's chilluns wuz small en eber New Y'ar Day,
we wuz put on a block en hired out ter de high bidduh, en
de money spent ter school de marster's chilluns."

"I wuz tole dat sum ob de white peeples wuz so mean ter
dere slaves dat de slaves would tek a pot en turn hit down
in a hollow ter keep dere whites fum yearin' dem singin'
en prayin'. De Ku Klux wuz bad on de ex-slaves at fust."

"De white folks 'fore de war had w'at dey called
"Muster" en I would go down wid dem. I would dance en de
folks would gib me money er gib me candy en durin' de war
de soldiers wuz de prettiest things."

"Got nuthin' at freedum en wuz not lookin' fuh nuthin'.
Ef marster had lived he might hab gib us sump'in. He wuz a

good man en good ter us. Eber since mah freedum, I'se wuk'd
as a laundress. Wuk'd fer one fam'ly ober 21 y'ars. 'Bout
two y'ars ago I lefted a tub, en hurt mahself. I'se not able
ter wuk now. I hab bin ma'ied twice en I'se voted three times."

"I went ter schul at Fisk, a short time, w'en hit wuz on
12th Avenue, but I diden' git ter go long 'nuff ter git en
edj'cation."

"Jis 'fore de Civil War I members de comet. Hit wuz
lak a big sta'r wid a long tail. Eve'body said hit wuz a
sign ob Judgement Day."

"Bad luck signs: Ef'n a picture falls, hit's a sign ob
de'th - bad luck ter step ovuh a broom - ef a clock stop
runnin' en later hit strike, dat means de'th."

"Sum ob de young peeple terday ez good but sum ob dem
don't wan'ter be nuthin'. De last war ruined mos' ob de
white en de black."

"I b'leeves in de Baptist 'ligion en 'longs ter de
Baptist Church, 9th Avenue N. en Cedar Street. De white
'oman I wuk'd fuh wan'ed me ter join de Christian (colored)
chuch. Only song I now members ez "On Jordans Banks I Stand."
"Don't think dis marrin' ob whites wid blacks should be
'lowed en think eve'y culor should stay ter hits-sef."

"I don't member now 'bout any stories tole back in ole
times. Our white folks wuz Christians en tried ter teach us
right en dey diden' tek up much time tellin' stories."

INTERVIEW

PATSY HYDE

504 9th Avenue N.

Nashville, Tennessee

"Dunno how ole I ez. I wuz bawn in slavery en b'longs
ter de Brown family. Mah Missis wuz Missis Jean R. Brown en
she wuz kin ter Abraham Lincoln en I useter y'ar dem talkin'
'bout 'im livin' in a log cabin en w'en he died she had her
house draped in black. Marster Brown wuz also good ter his
slaves. De Missis promus Marster Brown on his de'th bed
nebber ter let us be whup'd en she kep her wud. Sum ob de
oberseers on urthur plantations would tie de slaves ter a
stake en gib dem a good whup'in fer sump'in dey ought not ter
done."

"All cul'ed peeple wore cotton goods en de younger boys
run 'round in der shurt tails. Mah Missis nit all de white
chilluns stockin' en she made me sum. I had ter hold de yarn
on mah hans w'en she wuz nittin'. I members one time I wuz
keepin' flies off de table usin' a bunch ob peacock feathers
en I went ter sleep standin' up en she tole me ter go back ter
de kitchen." "I went en finish mah nap."

"One day ole Uncle Elick woke Marster Brown fum his
atter-noon nap tellin' 'im dat de prettiest men dat I ever seed
wuz passin' by on de road. He went ter de winder en said, "Good
Gawd, hit's dem damn Yankees." Mah white folks had a pretty

yard en gyarden. Soldiers kum en camped dere. I'd slip ter
de winder en lissen ter dem." "W'en dey wuz fightin' at Fort
Negley de cannons would jar our house. De Soldier's ban'
play on Capitol Hill, en play "Rally 'roun' de Flag Boys,
Rally 'roun de Flag."

"De slaves would tek dere ole iron cookin' pots en
turn dem upside down on de groun' neah dere cabins ter keep
dere white folks fum hearin' w'at dey wuz sayin'. "Dey claim-
ed dat hit showed dat Gawd wuz wid dem."

"In slavery time peeples b'leeved in dreams. I members
one nite I dreamed dat a big white thing wuz on de gatepost wid-
a haid. I tole mah mammy en she said, "Gawd wuz warning us."
De Ma'rige cer'mony in de days ob slavery wuz by de man en 'oman
jumpin' ovuh a broom handle tergedder."

"I don' member much 'boud de Ku Klux Klan, but I does
member seein' dem parade one time in Nashville." (She evident-
ly refers to the Klan's last parade in 1869 in Nashville,
immediately preceeding the disbandment of the Klan at Fort
Negley.).

"I members dat de northern soldier's ban' would play
Union Ferever, Rally 'roun de Flag, en Down Wid de Traitors
en up Wid de Star's en Stripes."

"De songs I members ez:

    I'se a Soldier ob de Cross.

    Follow de Lamb.

    I Would not Live Allus.

    I Axs not ter Stay.

Stars

"I member w'en de stairs fell. Hit wuz so dark en eberbody
wuz skeered, en I member a comet dat looked lak a big red ball
en had sump'in lak a tail on hit. Eber one wuz skeered en wuz
'feard hit would hit de groun' en burn de worl' up. I member
de fust street lites in Nashville. W'en de lamp mans would kum
'round en lite de lamps dey would yell out "all ez well" en I
also members de Southern money goin' out en Yankee money kum'n
in, en also w'en dere wuzn't any coal 'yer en eve'ythin' wuz wood
en mos' ob dis town wuz in de woods."

"De slaves wuz tole dey would git forty ak'rs ob groun' en a
mule w'en dey wuz freed but dey nebber got hit. W'en we wuz free
we wuz tuned out widout a thing. Mah grandmammy wuz an "Ole mammie"
en de Missis kep her. Atter freedum a lot ob Yankee niggah gals
kum down 'yer en hire out.

W'en I wuz a young girl hund'eds ob people went ter de wharf
at de foot ob Broadway on de fust Sunday in May ob eber'y year fer
de annual baptizin' ob new members inter de Baptist (culored) churches
ob de city. Thousands ob white people would crowd both sides ob de
Cumberland Riber, Broadway en de Sparkman Street Bridge ter witnus
de doin's. On leavin' de chuches de pastor would lead de parade ter
de wharf. Dey would sing en chant all de way fum de chuch ter de
river en sum ob de members would be ovuhkum wid 'ligious feelin' en
dey would hop up en down, singin' en shoutin' all de time, or may
be dey would start ter runnin' down de street en de brethern would
hab ter run dem down en bring dem back.

We useter hav' dem champ meetin's en dey wuz "honeys," en I
enjoy dem too. We wore bandanna handkerchiefs on our haids en long
shawls ovuh our shoulders. At dexe meetin's dey had all kinds ob
good things ter eat en drink.

"Atter mah freedum I dun washin' en Ironin' fer white families. Neber ma'ried but I neber worries no matter w'at happens en dat's may be cause ob mah livin' so long."

"Things ter day ez mighty bad. Not lak de ole days. Worl' ez gwin ter end soon."

"Atter I got ter feeble ter do washin' en ironin' fer mah livin', I went ter de Relief Office ter git dem ter he'ps me, but dey wouldn't do a thing. I had no place ter go er no money ter do wid. Dis culid 'oman tuk me in en does all she can fer me but now she ez disable ter wuk en I dunno w'at ter do. Ef'n I could git a small grocer order each week til I git de ole Age Pension hit would he'p lots."

INTERVIEW

ELLIS KEN KANNON

328 5th Avenue N.

St. Mary's Church

Nashville, Tennessee

"I dunno jes how ole I ez. I wuz bawn in Tennessee as a slave. Mah mammy kum frum Virginia. Our marster wuz Ken Kannon."

"Our Mistress wouldn't let us slaves be whup'd but I member mah daddy tellin' 'bout de Overseer whuppin' 'im en he run 'way en hid in a log. He tho't de blood hounds, he heered 'bout a half mile 'way, on his trail could heer 'im breathe but de hounds nebber fin' 'im. Atter de hounds pas' on, mah daddy lef' de log hidin' place en w'en he got ter a blacksmith shop, he se'ed a white man wid a nigger who had handcuffs on en w'en de white man tuk off de handcuffs, de nigger axed mah daddy whar he wuz gwine en he tole 'im back ter mah Mistress en de nigger sezs I ez too. Mah daddy slipped 'way fum 'im en went home."

"W'en I wuz a young boy, I didn't wear nothin' but a shirt lak all urthur boys en hit wuz a long thing lak a slip dat kum ter our knees. Our Mistress had a big fier place en w'en we would kum in cole she would say ain't you all cole. (You all was always used in the plural and not singular as some writers have it). W'ile we wuz warmin' she often played de organ fer us ter heer."

"I waited on mah Marster 'til he d'ed. Dey let me stay rite wid de body. Mah Mistress, Mammy ob de Marster, wuz in

bad health at dat time, en 'fore we sta'ted ter de graveyard,
I put a feather bed in de car'age en got a pitcher ob water
ready en 'fore we git dere she got awful sick."

"Durin' slavery de slaves hadder keep quiet en dey would
turn a kittle upside down ter keep de white folks 'yearin dere
prayers en chants. W'en a slave wanted ter go ter 'nother
plantation he had ter hab a pass. Ef' dey disobeyed dey got a
whuppin, en ef dey had a pass widout de Marsters signature dey
got a whuppin. Ef'n dey had ter hab passes now dere wouldin'
be no meaness."

"I member de Klu Klux Klan kumin ter mah daddy's home axin
fer water en dey would keep us totin' water ter dem fer fifteen
ter twenty minutes. Dey didn't whup er hurt any ob us. I also
member 'yearin mah mammy en daddy tellin' us 'bout de sta'rs
fallin'. I member de comet. Hit wuz a big ball en had a long
tail."

"I hab 'yerd dem tell 'bout Mr. Robertson. He wuz mean
ter his slaves en dey sezs dey could see a ball ob fier rollin'
on de fence en w'en dey would git ter de spring, a big white
thing lak a dog would crawl under de rock. De slaves wuz
natur'ally superstitious en b'leeved in dreams, ole sayings en
signs. I hab mahse'f se'ed things dat I ain't onderstan'. Hab
almost seen de things dat (apostle) John seed."

"Dunno nuthin 'bout any ob de ex-slaves voting er de Nat
Turner 'Bellion."

"Atter freedum mos' ob de slaves wuk'd fer dere livin' jes
as I ez. De men in de fiel's, de 'omen in de house. I wuk'd at
a hotel in McMinnville en one day, I wuz keepin' de flies off de
table wid a brush made frum fine strips ob papah en de string

broke en hit fell on de table. One man jumped up grabbed a cheer sayin' ah'll knock you down wid dis cheer."

"De slave 'pected ter git 40 akers ob land en a mule but nobody eber got hit as fur as I know. We didn't git nuthin. Our white peeple wuzzent able ter gib us anyting. Eve'ythin' dey had wuz tuk durin' de wah. Dey wuz good ter us en stuck wid us en mah peeple stayed wid mah Mistress."

"Dis young gineratshun ob niggers, I 'clare dey ez jes 'bout gon'. Dey won't wuk, all's stealin' en mabe wuk long 'nuff ter git a few clothes ter strut 'round in. I may be wrong but dat ez mah hones' pinion."

"De songs - I member ez:

    De Ole Ship ob Zion.
    Do You Think You'll be Able ter tek me Home."

"I has bin 'yer fifteen y'ars en hab wuked onder two Priests en now wukin under de third. Dey hab all bin nice ter me. Hab neber had any trubble wid white peeple en you'd be sprized how good dey ez ter me. Dey don't treat me lak a nigger."

"Eber since I got mah freedum en 'fore I got dis chuch job, I dun all kinds ob odd jobs, waited on tables, pressin' clothes en anyting else dat kum 'long, but sum jobs wuz small pay but hit kep me 'live."

"Don't member any slave uprisin's. Our peeple wuz good ter us."

INTERVIEW

SCOTT MARTIN

438 Fifth Ave., No.

"I'se 90 y'ars ole and wuz bawn in slavery in Sumner County, Tennessee and I b'long to Marster Dr. Madison Martin an' mah Misses Mary. And I wuk'd wid de stock an' wuz de houseman."

"I hab neber been in any truble, neber 'rested en neber bin in jail. I knows how ter behave, but de young peeples ob terday ain' dun rite en dey don' 'mounts ter much. Dar am a few dat am all rite. In de ole days dey wer' bettuh dan dey ez terday. De white and black ougher not ma'rie."

"I has voted two times, but I disremembers who I voted fer. Neber hadney frens in office en I nebr met any of de Klu Klux men. I didn' go out much en I neber wuz kotched w'en I did git out. I heered lots 'bout nigger uprisin' but dey wuz away off."

"I b'long ter de Missionary Baptist chuch an' I useter preach in mah chuch 'ouse en udders w'en called. Once a y'ar I wud be at de Cumberland Riber wha'f en' baptiz' culled peeples all da'. We useter hab camp meetin' in de ole days en hab good things ter eat en I would preach all day. I went ter schul two sessions en den I went to wuk."

"I member de fust street kar line that run on East side of Cumberland Riber ter East end ob de ole wood bridge dat de 'arly settlers build. De kars wer' pulled by hosses

en' mules. De whites en blacks mixed tergedder en den de
law made de whites rid' in frunt en the blacks in de rearuh.
I think dat wuz rite, but sum ob mah race wuz mad 'bout hit.
I wuz on a kar one day and mules run'd 'way en de ole red
mule got loose frum de kar en run'd ober a mile 'fore dey
ketched him en dey brot 'im ba'k en de kar' pas' on. I
members de ole L & N Railroad on de East side. W'en my folks
wud ride de train dey had 'ter hold me tite or I wuld git
'way frum dem en run en hide 'hind sum logs. I wuz scar'et
ter ride on de kars."

"Atter freedum de slaves had'n no truble ter go whar
dey wan'. Menny lef' but menny stay wid der ole marsters.
I stay wid my marster tell he d'ed. I den kum an' lib wid
mah daddy on Lebanon Road. Atter dat I libed on Gallatin
Road an' den I kum ter Nashville, an' wuk wid pic' and shovel
on streets, sewers an' udder jobs. I heered dem sez dat de
slaves wud git lan', hoss, money er sumpin'but I neber heerd
ob nobody gittin nuthin'. Dere wuz not slave 'raisings eroun'
whar I wuz."

"De fallin' st'ars wuz 'fore mah time, but I'se heer'd
mah daddy tole 'bout hit. I se'd de comet wid hit shinnin'
tail an' I fust b'leevd sumbody put hit up dere."

"Good luck sign wuz w'en a stray cat kum ter yo' house
an' stay dere. Bad luck sign wuz a black kat crossin' yo'
path in frunt ob yer. Ter ke'p frum havin' de bad luck yo
back up pas' whar hit crossed yer path en den spit an' yer
hab no bad luck."

"Dem air ships luk nice but dey ez spoke 'boud in de
Holy Bible, dat sum day dere wud be flyin' things in de
air'h an' I think dat dese things am it. De otomobeels kiver
nuder passag' in de Bible which seze de peeple 'll rid' on
de streets widout hosses en mules."

"Mah fav'rite songs am "I Gwine to Jine de Gideon
Band," and "Keep Yo' Lits Bunnin'."

"Ter ole now ter wuk an' mah haid don' se'm ter be
tergedder an' I'se gits he'ps frum de Welfare."

410012

INTERVIEW

ANN MATTHEWS

719 9th Ave. South

Nashville, Tennessee

"I wuz bawn in Murfreesboro on Stones River. I dunno
how ole I ez en hit meks me 'shamed ter tell peeple dat, but
mah mammy would hit me in de mouth w'en I'd ax how ole I
wuz. She say I wuz jes' tryin' ter be grown."

"Mah mammy's name wuz Frankie en mah daddy wuz Henry Ken
Kannon. Don' member much 'bout mah mammy 'cept she wuz a sho't
fat Indian 'oman wid a turrible tempah. She d'ed, durin' de war,
wid black measles."

"Mah daddy wuz part Indian en couldn't talk plain. W'en
he go ter de store he'd hab ter put his han' on w'at he want
ter buy. He d'ed eight months 'fore de Centennial."

"Our marster en missis wuz Landon en Sweenie Ken Kannon.
Dey wuz good ter us, en we had'n good things ter eat."

"I member de Yankee en Southern soldiers. One day me
en mah young missis, en sum chilluns went up ter de road en we
se'ed sum Yankee soldiers kumin', I clum'ed on de fence, de
urthurs run 'way en hid. One ob de soldiers sezs ter me,
'Lettle girl who wuz dat wid you,' en I sezs, 'Hit wuz Miss Puss
en sum chilluns.' He laughed en sezs, 'You ez brave ain' you?'"

"Our missis let us go ter chuch. I 'long ter de chuch
ob Christ."

"I dunno ob but one slave dat got lan' er nothin' w'en
freedum wuz 'clared. We didn't git nuthin at freedum. Mah
daddy went back in de woods en built us a saplin house en

dobbed hit wid mud. Atter freedum mah daddy went 'way, en we chilluns staid in dat house in de woods by oursel's. Dere wuz two weeks we didn't see a bit ob bre'd. I went up w'at ez called de nine mile cut neah Tullahoma, en axed a 'oman ef she would let us hab sum bre'd. She gib me sum meat en bre'd, en tole me ter kum back. I went back home en we et sump'in, en I went back ter de 'oman's house, she gib me a sack ob flour en a big piece ob midlin' meat. We wuz skeered, bein' dere 'lone so I would set up wile mah br'ers slep', den I'd sleep in de daytime. One nite sumbody knocked at de do'er en hit wuz mah daddy en he had two sacks ob food, en de urthur chilluns got up en we et a big meal."

"I useter 'yer de folks talk 'bout de sta'rs fallin', but dat happen' 'fore I wuz bawn."

"I didn't go ter schul, mah daddy wouldin' let me. Said he needed me in de fiel wors den I needed schul. I wuz allus sassy en stubbun. I run 'way fum mah daddy en kum ter Nashville. I stayed at a schul on Franklin Pike, run by Mrs. McGathey. I wuz de only cul'ed person dere. Dey wuz good ter me en eve'y Chrismus I would git a big box ob clothes en things."

"In Manchester de Klu Klux Klan wore big high hats, red handkerchiefs on dere faces en red covers on dere hosses. Dey tuk two niggers out ob jail en hung dem ter a chestnut tree."

"One nite w'en I wuz gwine wid mah daddy fum de fiel' home, we met sum ob de K.K.K. en dey said, 'Ain't you out late Henry? En who ez dat gal wid you?' Mah daddy said, 'We ez gwine home fum wuk, en dis ez mah daughter.' Dey said, 'Whar has she bin, we ain't nebber se'ed her.' He told dem, 'I'd bin in Nashville.' Dey said dey'd be back dat nite but we didn't see dem."

"W'en I wuz in Manchester I promus de Lawd I wouldin' dance. But one nite I wuz on de ball floor, dancin' fum one end ob de room ter de urthur en sump'in sezs go ter de do'er, I didn't go right den en 'gin hit sezs you ez not keepin' yo promus. I went ter de do'er en you could pick a pin off de groun' hit wuz so light. In de sky wuz de prettiest thing you ebber se'ed, so many culors, blue, white, green, red en yellow."

"Since freedum I'se wuked wid diff'ent peeple, cookin' en keepin' house. I'se de mammy ob three chilluns. Two ob dem ez 'way fum 'yer, en I live 'yer wid mah daughter."

"Old songs, I member ez:

Dark wuz de Nite.
I'll Live wid Gawd Forever, Bye en Bye.
Fum dis Earth I go, Oh Lawd, W'at Will 'kum ob Me."

"So yer wan't me ter tell you de truf? I think de young peeple ez nothin'. Dey think dey ez smaht. Most ob de ex-slaves I'se knowed has cooked en nussed, done laundry wuk; wuked in fiel's en diff'ent things."

"I'se neber voted en hab neber paid any 'tention ter de niggers gittin' ter vote. Don't hab any frens in political office. Can't member any tales er signs."

"I don't b'leeve in dese mixed white and black families en hit shouldn't be 'lowed."

"Durin' slavery de white folks didn't want de niggahs ter sing en pray, but dey would turn a pot down en meet at de pot in de nite en sing en pray en de white folks wouldn't 'yer dem."

"Ef a slave d'ed de white folks wouldn't let no body set up wid de body 'cept de niggers ob dat plantation, but urthur slaves would slip in atter dark, set up en den slip back ter dere plantation 'fore day."

"W'en I useter go ter camp meetin' dey had big dinnahs en spread hit on de groun'. Dey preached, sung, shouted en eve'ybody had a good time."

"Fum de camp meetin's dey would go ter de wharf en baptize. Dey would tie handkerchiefs 'roun dere haids. W'en dey wuz dipped under de water sum ob dem would kum up shoutin'."

A TALE

One time de preacher wuz in de river fixin' ter baptize a man. Eve'ybody wuz singin' ole time 'ligion. A 'oman sung, "I don' lak dat thing 'hind you." Bout dat time de pahson en de udder man se'd an alligator. De parson sezs, "No-By-God I Don't Either." He turned de man loose en dey both run 'way.

INTERVIEW

REV. JOHN MOORE

809 7th Avenue So.

Nashville, Tennessee

"I wuz bawn in Georgia (exact time not known) en mah mammy wuz half Indian en mah daddy a slave. Both ob dem owned by William Moore. Sum time atter dat Marster Moore sold mah daddy en den de Moore Sistuhs looked atter me en wuz allus good ter me. "Lawdy, dey wuz good white folks."

"Durin' slavery times de slaves would hab ter git fum dere marster a pas' 'fore dey could visit dere own peeple on de uther plantations. Ef'n you had no pass you would git in trouble ef caught wid out one which allus ment a good whuppin' w'en dey returned. At dat time menny slaves would run 'way en hide in caves en menny ob dem would go by de "ondergroun' railroad" ter Canada whar slavery wuz not recognized." (The underground railroad consisted of hiding places throughout the states to Canada and the slaves would make the trip under cover from station to station.)"

"De slaves would slip out at nite ter private meetin's en turn a pot bottom up on de groun' en leave a little hole under hit so de sound ob dere talkin' would go onder de pot en no one would 'year whut dey wuz talkin' 'bout.

"De ex-slaves ob de better class did vote en de white peeple stuck wid de good cul'ed folks. I don' member now 'bout de Nat Turner 'Bellion."

"Atter freedum de slaves wuz 'lowed ter stay on de plantation en 'lowed ter farm en gib half dey made. Atter slavery I useter wuk fer fifty cents en git a peck ob meal, three pounds ob bacon en a quart ob syrup which would las' a week."

"De Ku Klux Klan's plan wuz ter whup all white er cul'ed peeple dat didn't stay at home en support dere families but would run 'roun en live a bad life. W'en de Klan would be passin' through de slaves would call dem ghostus."

"One nite mah br'er en me wuz sleepin' in de dining room. Sumpin woke us en we seed sumpin' dat kum through de yard en got hold ob sum blocks. Dat thing didn't hab no haid en didn't hab no tale en looked lak hit wuz backin' up on all four legs. Nex mawnin' we could fin' no tracks ob whuteber hit wuz en de gate wuz also fasened."

"Dis young peeples 'cordin' ter de Bible ez on de broad road ter ruin. Dey think dey ez as good as de white peeple but dey ez classed as niggahs in mah eyes."

"Caint member any ob de ole songs now."

Andrew Moss
88 Auburn Streets
Knoxville,Tennessee

"One ting dat's all wrong wid did world today," according to Andrew

Moss,aged negro, as he sits through the winter days before an open grate fire

in his cabin,with his long ,lean fingers clasped over his crossed knees, "is

dat dey ain no 'prayer grounds'. Down in Georgia what I was born, -dat was 'way

back in I852,- us colored folks had prayer grounds. My Mammy's was a ole

twisted thick-rooted muscadine bush. She'd go in dar and pray for deliverance

of de slaves. Some colored folks cleaned out knee-spots in de cane breaks.Cane

you know, grows high and thick, and colored folks could hide de'seves in dar,

an nobody could see an pester em."

      "You see it was jes like did. Durin' de war, an befo de war too, white

folks make a heap o fun of de colored folks for alltime prayin. Sometime,say,

you was a slave en you git down to pray in de field or by de side of de road.

White Marster come 'long and see a slave on his knees.He say,"What you prain'

'bout?" An you say,'Oh,Marster I'se jes prayin' to Jesus cause I wants to go

to Heaven when I dies.' An Marster say,' Youse my negro.I git ye to Heaven.Git

up off'n your knees.' De white folks what owned slaves thought that when dey

go to Heaven de collored folk's would be dar to wait on em.   An ef'n it was

A Yank come 'long, he say too,"What you prain' 'bout?' You gives de same

'sponse. An he say," We'se gwine save you.We goin' to set you free.You wants

to be free,dont you?' 'Yessir,Boss!'.'well den,Yank say, come go 'long wid

me.' Ain no use keep sayin' ' please sir Boss,I'll have to arsk my Master.'

Yank say,'what you mean ,Marster? You aint got no Marster.We's settin' you

free.'"

" Sometimes day takes a\ tie a rope 'round you, and they starts ridin'
off but dey dont go too fas' so you walks behind. Sometimes 'long comes
another Yank on a horse an he arsk,'Boy ain you tired?' 'Yessir Boss! 'Well
den you git up here behind me and ride some.' Den he wrop de rope all 'round
de saddle horn.Wrops andWrops, but leaves some slack.But he keeps you tied,so's
you wont jump down and run away. An many's de time a prayin' negro got took off
like dat, and want never seen no more."

"'Course ef'n you goes wid em,you ' member your trainin' and 'fore you
leaves de field, you stacks your hoe nice, like you was quittin' de days work.
Dey learned the little'uns to do dat,soon's dey begins to work in de fields.
Dey had little hoes, handles 'bout de size of my arm,for de little fellers.
I've walked many a mile, when I was a little feller,up and down de rows,
followin' de grown folks, an chopping wid de hoe 'round de corners whar de
earth was soft so de little uns could hoe easy. Whoopee! Let dat dinner horn
blow, and evy body stacks dey hoes, nince,neat stacks standin up, and starts
to run. Some eats in dey own cabins, but dem what eats at de big house, sets
 down at a long table, and gets good grub too! Evy night, our Marster give
us evy one a glass o whiskey.Dat's to keep off decease. Mornins' we had to
all drink tar water for de same purpose.Dat want so tasty."

"My Marster's name was George Hopper.Dat man paid taxes on more'n
two-thousand acres of land in two counties. I lived in them two counties.Was
born in Wilkes and raised in Lincoln County,Georgia. We called it de middle-
south. My Marster he never did marry.Lots of folks didnt, dey jes took up wid
one another. Marster Hopper had five children by my grandmother.She was his
house woman, dat's what he call 'er. An when he died he willed her an all dem
chilluns a house, some land , and a little money.He'd of left em a heap more
money and ud been one the richest men in the country, ef'n de war hadnt broke out.
When it was over he had a barrel full of 'federate greenbacks.But t'want no count.

He done broke den. One day my uncle, he was the colored overseer, he went to Danbury, six miles from whar we lived at, and he paid $5 for a pound of coffee. Dat was befo de North whupped de South, and dey had'n killed-down de money value for de South."

"Talk about hard times! We see'd em in dem days, durin' de war and most specially after de Surrender. Folks dese days dont know what trouble looks like. We was glad to eat ashe-cakes and drink parched corn and rye 'stead o Coffee. I've seed my grandmother go to de smoke house, and scrape up de dirt whar de meat had drapped, and take it to de house fer seasonin. You see, both armies fed off'n de white folks, and dey cleaned out dey barns and cellars and smoke houses when dey come. One time, when de Yanks was on de way to Augusta, I was picking up chips to make the supper fire, when I see'd em comin'. I hit it out from dar and hide behind two little hills down by de big spring. After awhile my brother find me and he tell me to come on back to the house and see dem white mens dance. De Yanks kep' comin' and dey eat all night. By daylight they was through marchin past."

" An den come de Rebels. When dey come we had five-thousand bushel of corn, one-hundred head o hogs, three-hundred and fifty galons of syrup 'en sech. When dey left,　they took an set fire to evything, to keep it away from the Yanks, aimin to starve em out o dat country. Dat's what dey done. Some of dem Rebs was mean as the Yanks. And dat was bein' mean. Some called de Yanks, 'de Hornets', 'cause dey fight so. Take a Yank an he'd fight acrost a buzz saw and it circlin' fifty mile a minute."

" Dat time when the Yanks was goin' to Augusta, an I went to black my Marster's boot,—he'd give us a two-cent peice, big as a quarter- for boot blackin, I say, 'Marster who is dem soldiers?' An he say to me, 'Dey's de Yankees, come to try to take you away from me.' 'n I say, "Looks like to me Marster, ef'n dey wants to take us dey'd ask you fer us.' Marster laughed and say, 'Boy! Dem fellers dont axes wid words. Dey does all dey talkin' wid cannons.'

Did you know that a white woman shot de first cannon dat was ever fired in de

state o Georgia? She was a Yankee Colonel's wife,dey say, named Miss Anna,I

dunno the rest o her name. She wants to be de first to fire a cannon she say,

to set the negroes free. Dat was afore' de war, begin. De roar of dat cannon

was in folkes ears for more'n five days and nights. "

       Uncle Andrew gave a little grunt as he lifted himself out of his chair.

His little frame seemed lost in the broadshouldered lumber jacket that he wore.

He had laid aside the paper sack from which he had been eating,when the visitor

came, and removed an old stocking cap from his head. When the visitor suggested

that he keep it on, as he might catch cold he replied,"I dont humor myself none."

The sunlight fell upon his head and shoulders as he stood, to steady himself on

his feet.Traces of his ancestry of Indian blood,-one of his grandfathers was

a Cherokee Indian,- were evident in his features. His skin is jet-black,but his

forehead high and his nose straight, with nostrils only slightly full. There was

dignity in his bearing and beauty in his face,with its halo of cotton-white

hair and beard,cut short and neatly parted in the middle of his chin.

       Walking about the room,he called the visitors attention to family por-

traits on the walls.Some were colored crayons, and a few ere enlarged snap-

shots. Proudly he pointed to the photograph of a huge-sized Negro man,apparently

in his thirties, and said,"He was our first comins' Reckon he took after his

great granddaddy, who was eight feet tall and weighed twe-hundred and fifty

pounds. That man's arms was so long, when dey hung down by his side, his fingers

was below his knees. This grandfather was free-born.My father,Dave Moss, he was

sold three times. He had twenty-five children. But he had two wives. As I

aforesaid, folks didnt always marry in dem days,jes took up wid one another.

My mother was his title-wife. By her, he jes had me and my two full-brothers

an one sister. My mother died two years after the war. My father give my

sister to my grandmother.Jes give ' er to 'er."

" How come I live in Knoxville, I was a young man, when I started off from Georgia, aimin to go over de mountains to Kentucky whar I heard dey pay good wages. I stopped in Campbell country,Tennessee wid another feller, and I see'd a pretty gal workin' in de field. An I say's,I'm goin' to marry dat gal. Sho 'nough me an her was married in less dan six months. Her Marster built me a log house and we lived dar 'till we come to Knoxville,Tennessee. Now, all o my boys is dead.Evy one o em worked for Mr.Peters (Peters and Bradley Flour Mills, of Knoxville)- and dey all died worin' fer him. So Mister Willie, he say he gwine let me live here, in de company house, the rest o my days."

The four room frame house stands near a creek at the dead end of an alley on which both whites and negroes live.The huge double bed ,neatly made, stands between two windows from which there is an unobstructed view of the highway traversing north and south through northern Knoxville, several blocks away from Andrew's home. "I jes lay down on dat bed nights and watch them autimobiles flyin by. Dey go Blip! Blip!and Blip! An I say to my self,'Watch them fools! ' Folkes ain got de sense dey's born wid.Ain smart like dey used to be.An times ain good like dey was. Ef'n it hadnt been for some of dem crazy fools, actin up and smarty, me an my wife'd be gittin maybe a hun'ered an' more dollars a month,'stead o the fifteen we gits 'tween us for ole' age help. They'd ought to let Rosevelt alone.An its his own folks as is fitin' 'im.He is a big man even ef he is a Democrat. I'm a Republican though. Voted my first time for Blaine."

"Yes I votes sometimes now, when dey come gits me. An befo I got sick, I would ride the street car to town.An I goes down to de Court House, and when I see dem cannons in deyard I cain keep from cryin'. My wife arsk me what make me go look at dem cannon ef'n dey makes me cry.An I tells her I cain't cry'bout de good and de bad times dem cannon bringed us.But no cannons or nothin' else, seems like going to bring back de good old times.But I dont worry 'bout all dese things much.Accordin' to de Good Book's promise, weepin' may endure for a night, den come joy in de mornin. An I knows dat de day's soon come when I goes

to meet my folks and my Lord an Marster in his Heaven, whar dey ain no more

weepin.'

                              # # #

SUBJECT- EX-SLAVE STORIES

Aunt Mollie Moss
88- Auburn Street,
Knoxville,Tennessee

There is no street sign or a number on any of the ramshackled frame
cottages that seemingly lean with the breezes, first one direction, then another, along the alley that wind's through the city's northernmost boundary
and stops its meanderings at the doorstep of "Uncle Andrew Moss" and his wife,
"Aunt Mollie."

The City Directory of Knoxville,Tennessee officially lists the Moss
residence as # 88 Auburn Street. It rests upon its foundations more substan-
tially, and is in better kept condition than its neighbors. In lieu of a
"reg8lar" house number, the aged negro couple have placed a rusty automobile
lisence tag of ancient vintage conspicuously over their door. It is their
jesture of contempt for their nearest white neighbors who " dont seem to care
whedder folkses know whar dey lib an maybe don wants em to."

As for Aunt Mollie, she holds herself superior to all of her neighbors. She "Ain got no time for po white trash noway." She shoo'ed two little
tow-headed white girls from her doorstep with her broom as she stood in her
door and watched a visitor approach."G'wan way frum here now,can be bodder
wid you chillun messin ups my front yard.Take yo tings an go on back to yo
own place!"

"Dats way dey do," she mumbled as she lead the visitor inside the
cottage,through the dining-room and kitchen into the living-room and bedroom.
"Don know what I gwine do when come summer time.Keeps me all time lookin out
for dem chilluns.Dey's dat troublesome. Brings trash in on my flo what I jes
scoured, an musses 'roun, maybe tryin to steal sumpin an me watchin em too.
Dey wasnt teached manners an 'havior in odder folkses houses like what I war."

Aunt Mollie Moss,
88 Auburn St,Knoxville,Tenn

When Aunt Mollie learned that it was to hear her story of how she was
trained in manners and behaviorism, that the visitor had come, and to hear
something of her recollections of slave days, her belligerent mood vanished.
The satisfied manner in which she drew up chairs before the fire, take a pinch
of snuff and settle her skirts, indicated that was going to be quite a session.
She leaned her elbows on her knees, held her head between the palms of her
hands and fumbled in her cloudy memory to gather a few facts to relate.

Uncle Andrew,the more intelligent of the two, and quick to seize upon
his opportunity,began his reminiscences immediately, saying "Honey, wait now,"
when his wife thought herself well organized to talk, and frequently broke into
his narrative."Wait untell I gits through.Den you can talk." Aunt Mollie would
frown and grunt,mumble to herself as she rocked back and forth in her chair.
She pulled the two long braids of brown silky hair, streaked with white, and
tied at the ends with cotton strings. She spat vigorously into the fire,kept
muttering and shuffling her feet,which were encased in men's shoes.

At last it came Aunt Mollie's turn to talk war-times.Uncle Andrew,well
pleased with his recital, retired to his corner by the hearth and listened
"mannardly" - after first warning the visitor in a gentle undertone, that"My
wife she ain got much mem'ry an she don hear good." Aunt Mollie's rambling
reminiscences backed up his statement. She began.

" Reckon I mus be 'bout eighty-two,three year old. I dunno exactly.
Ef I knowed whar to find em, deys some my white folkes lib in dis town.Seem like
I can 'member dey names. I b'longed to Marster Billy Cain, and was raised on
his farm in Campbell county,Tennessee. Oh,'bout six,seven mile from Jacksboro.
Wish I could go back dar some time. Ain been dar sence me an Moss married an
live eight,ten or some more years in a log cabin he built for us. We was
married March 7, de day atter Cleveland was ' lected presi-dent. In 1885 did

you say ? Well, reckon you're right. I ain had no schoolin an I can 'member
lots o tings I used to know."

"Billy Cain worked me in de fields. An his wife Miss Nancy say she
gwine stop it,'cause I was so pretty she fraid somebody come stel me." Aunt
Mollie buried her face in her apron and had a good laugh. "Dey said I was
de pretties girl anywhars about.Had teeth jes like pearls.Whoops.Look at em
now. Ain got 'nuff left to chaw wid. You notices how bright-complected I is?
My own father was a full-blooded Cherokee indian. De Yanks captured him an
killed him."

" I was hoein in de field dat time Moss com 'long and see me and say
he gwine marry me. An,jes like he tell you, we was married in less dan six months.
We been livin togedder evy since and we gits along good.We have had blessins'
and got a lot to be thankful for. Could have more to eat sometimes,but we gits
along someways. I am a good cook. Miss Nancy she teached me all kinds o cookin,
puttin up berries,makin pickles and bakin bread and cake an evy'ting. Her ole
man Cain give us good grub dem days.Monday mornins we go to de Cains to git
rations for de week. Dey gib us three pounds wheat, a peck o meal, a galon o
molasses, two pound o lard, two pound o brown sugar, rice an evy'ting. I use to
have plates an china white folks gib me. White woman come one day,say she wan
buy 'em. Took plum night all I had.Did'n pay me much o nothin' either."

"Yes,Lord. I does 'member 'bout de war. I've see'd de blue an I've see'd
de grey. In 1862 I see'd de soldiers formin' in line.I was a great big girl.
Dem swords glisen' like stars. Can'member whar dey was goin dat time. But I
ain forgit de times soldiers come foragin. Dey got all dey wanted, too,Hep'
dey sef's an dont pay for it, never. Soldier see a chicken go under de house,
he plop down and shoot , and den call me to crawl under de house and fetch it
out." Aunt Mollie buried her head in her apron again and laughed like a child.
"Lordy how scared I was of de old gander dat blowed at me,whilst I was tryin'
to drag'em out alive, when I see'd de soldiers comin'."

" Billy Cain, he was brudder-in-law to Old Townslee, who lived on a plantation in Alabama. How come my mother was   give to Cain an come to Tennessee, was one mornin' Old Townslee rode his horse out under a tree to blow up de slaves.Blow de horn you know,to call 'em to work. Somebody shot 'im. Right off his horse. It was so dark, 'fore daylight, and couldnt see and dey never did find out who shot 'im. Heap o white folks had enemies dem days. So de slaves he owned was divided munxt his chilluns. My mother was one of nine dat come to Billy Cain dat way."

"Talk 'bout your shootin jest for devilment. Lemme tell you 'bout old man John Wynn.He live down dar 'bout ten mile from whar Moss lived when he was a boy.I've heard em tell it many a time. Dey say John Wynn had 185 slaves. Evy time it come George Washington's birthday, Old Wynn he had a feast and invite all de slaves!He celebraten! he say. He seta a long table wid all kind good tings to eat. An he count de slaves,so's to be sure dey all come. An' den he'd take an pick out one and shoot him! Den he say,"Now youse all can go'head an eat.Throw dat nigger'sidd an we bury im in mornin'." And he walks off to de big house. No! He wasnt drunk . Jes de debil in 'im. Well, he shot ten, twelve, maybe thirty dat way.An den de white folks hanged 'im to a tree.Hanged im t'well he was good and dead,dey did."

"Now folkes can 'joy dey victuals wid sech goin's on. De slaves git so's dey scared to hear de bell ring.   Don' know what it mean.Maybe death,maybe fire, maybe nudder sale o some body.Gwine take'em way. But when de bell ring dey had to come.Let dat ole bell ring and de woods was full o negroes.Maybe 500 hundred come from all over date county."

Aunt Mollie was beginning to ramble amd babble incoherently, her memories of her own and the experiences of others all confused in her mind. When she had about finished a story about how one of the slave women,"bust de skull" of the head of her marster,'" 'cause she was missin a sick baby an' he tell her she got

Aunt Mollie Moss,
88 Auburn Street,
Knoxville, Tennessee

to git out in dat field an hoe" and the gory details of what the shovel did to

the white marster's head, it was time for the visitors to close the interview.

Both Uncle Andrew and Aunt Mollie followed the visitor to the front

door, and wished her "All de luck in de world. An thank you for comin' An

come see us agin, nudder time."

# # #

INTERVIEW

ANDY ODELL

1313 Pearl Street

Nashville, Tennessee

"I wuz bawn east ob Spring Hill, Tennessee. I dunno
in w'at y'ar, but I wuz a ful' grown man w'en I wuz freed.
(This will make him about 96 years old.). I wuz an onlies'
chile en I nebber knowed mah daddy. Mah mammy wuz sold 'way
fum me. She ma'ied a man named Brown en dey had seven
chillun."

"At fust I 'longed ter Marster Jim Caruthers. W'en
his daughter ma'ied Fount Odell, I wuz willed ter her en
den mah marsters wuz Fount en Albert Odell who wuz br'ers.
Mah white folks let us go ter chuch. I b'leeves in de Baptist
'ligion. I nebber knowed any slave dat had ter hide ter sing
er pray. I members de comet en hit wuz a sta'r wid a long
tail en looked lak hit wuz burnin'. De sta'rs fell 'fore I
wuz bawn." (The stars fell in 1833).

"We had ter hab passes en if you didn't hab one, you
got whupped. Mah marster let me go ter chuch wid' out a
pass. I members de Klu Klux Klan but dey nebber bothered
me, tho I 'yeard a lot 'bout dem. Dey called demselves
"White Caps" en said dey wuz rite fum de grave. W'en a slave
got whupped hit wuz cose dey disobey dere white folks en de
overseer whupped dem. I though mah white folks wuz awful mean
ter me sumtime."

"I nebber b'leeved in ghos' but hab yeard lots 'bout dem.
Lots of peeples did b'leeve in dem back in dem times. Uster

sing a lot but I dunno names ob dem now. I dunno w'at ez gwine
ter 'kum ob dis young crowd. I sho don't think diff'ent culers
oughter ma'rie. De Lawd didn't mean fer hit ter be dun. Dunno
ob any slave 'risin's in Virginia er any uther place. Don't
member now de tales en sayin' ob de ole times."

"Member well w'en de war broke out en how dey had big
dinners en marched 'round ovuh de fiel's, gittin' ready fer
de war. I had a br'er kilt in de war en mah mammy got a
lettle money fum 'im. Also member dat w'en mah mammy got de
money she bought me a hat."

"I don't git nuthin at freedum en I dunno ob any slaves
gittin' any land er money. I know dat w'en we wuz freed Marster
Albert called us slaves in en said, "You all ez as free as I ez,
but you can stay 'yer en wuk fer me ef'n you want ter." I staid
wid 'im a good w'ile atter freedum."

"Since freedum I hab plowed, hoed, cut wood, en wuk'd in
quarries pecking rock. Hab nebber wuk'd in town fer I dunno
de things 'bout town. I hab voted almost eve'y election since
freedum 'til dese last few years. I hab had two frens in office
but both ez de'd now. I uster think 'omen shouldn't vote, but I
guess hit ez alri'te.

INTERVIEW

LAURA RAMSEY PARKER

715 Gay St.

Nahhville, Tennessee

"I'se 87 y'ars ole. Wuz bawn in slavery. Wuz freed
w'en de slavery stopped. Mack Ramsey wuz mah marster en
he wuz sho good ter his slaves. He treated dem as human
bein's. W'en he turned his slaves 'loose he gib dem no
money, but gib dem lands, clothin' en food 'til dey could
brang in dere fust crop. Mah daddy rented a strip ob land
'til he wuz able ter buy de place. He lived on de same fer
menny y'ars."

"W'en I wuz ole er'nuff I wuz taught ter spin en weav.
I bucum de nuss ter de marster's onlies' chile. Soon atter
I wuz freed, I went ter Wisconsin, but only wuz dere fer a
y'ar, den I kum back ter Tennessee en Nashville. I settled
in dis house en I'se bin livin' in hit fer ovuh fifty y'ars.
Dere wuz no uther houses 'round 'yer at de time. I own de
place. Hab wuk'd all mah life seem ter me. At one time I
wuz a chambermaid at de Nicholson House now de Tulane en
later 'kum a sick nuss, a seamstress, dressmaker but now I
pieces en sells bed quilts. I does mah own housekeepin' en
washin'."

"I don't member now, very much 'bout de Ku Klux Klan. I
do member dat one nite dey passed our home en I grab'ed a
shotgun en said dat I wuz gwine ter shoot dem ef dey kum on
de place. I members de Battle ob Murfreesboro, but I'se

got no membrances ob any slave uprisin'."

"I think very lettle ob de younger ginerashon. Dere's many things ter day dat should be changed, but I'se 'yer en can't do nuthin' ter change hit. I's min'in mah own business. I puts mah faith en trust in Gawd's han's; en treats mah nabers right; en lives honest. I 'longs ter de Christian Chuch, but don't wan'ter be called a "Campbellite."

"De songs I members ez:

Am I a Soldier ob de Cross.

Am I Bawn ter Die?

'Tis 'Ligion Dat Can Gib."

INTERVIEW

NAISY REECE

710 Overton St.

Nashville, Tennessee

"I wuz bawn in slavery, in Williamson County, guess
I'se 'bout 80 y'ars ole. Think I wuz fou' w'en de wah
started."

"Mah mammy en daddy wuz Mary en Ennock Brown."

"Mah missis en marster wuz Polly en Randall Brown."

"Dunno ob any ob our fam'ly bein' sold. W'en freedum
wuz declar' we wuz tu'n loose wid nothin'. Mah daddy tuk us
down in de kuntry, raised crops en made us wuk in de fiel'."

"I'se cooked a leetle fer urther peeple, but mos' ob
mah wuk has bin laundry. I didn't go ter schul much. I
dunno w'at ter say 'bout de younger gineratshun; dere ez sich
a diff'unce now ter w'at hit wuz w'en I wuz a girl. Dunno
any tales dat I useter 'year."

"Didn't see any Klu Klux Klan, but I alluz got skeered
en hid w'en we'd 'year dey wuz kumin'. I 'long ter de Baptist
Church. I neber want ter menny camp-meetin's, but went ter
a lot ob baptizins."

"Mammy tole us how de sta'rs fell en how skeered ebery-
body got. I saw de long tail comet."

Signs: "Good luck ter git up 'fore day-lite ef'n youer
gwin sum place er start sum wuk." "Bad luck ter sweep flo'

atter dark en sweep de dirt out."

    <u>Songs</u>:   "I Couldn't Hear Anybody Pray."
               "Ole Time 'Ligion."
               "Cross De Riber Jordan."

"I'se neber voted, en hab neber had any frens in office. Neber knowed nothin' 'bout de slave mart er de 'structshun days."

INTERVIEW

MILLIE SIMPKINS

"BLACK MAMIE"

1004 10th Avenue, No.

Nashville, Tennessee

I claims I's 109 ye'ars ole en wuz bawn neah Winchester,
Tennessee. Mah marster wuz Boyd Sims en mah missis wuz Sarah
Ann Ewing Sims. Mah mammy wus named Judy Ewing en mah daddy
wuz Moses Stephens en he wus "free bawn." He wuz de marster's
stable boy en followed de races. He run 'way en nebber kum
back.

Mah fust missis wuz very rich. She had two slave 'omen ter
dress her eve'y mawnin' en I brought her breakfust ter her on a
silvah waitah. She wuz ma'ied three times, her second husband
wuz Joe Carter en de third wuz Judge Gork.

Mah fust millis sold me kaze I wuz stubborn. She sent me ter
de "slave yard" aat Nashville. De yard wuz full ob slaves. I stayed
dere two weeks 'fore marster Simpson bought me. I wuz sold 'way
fum mah husband en I nebber se'd 'im 'gin. I had one chile which I
tuk wid me.

De slave yard wuz on Cedar Street. A Mr. Chandler would bid
de slaves off, but 'fore dey started biddin' you had ter tek all ob
ye Clothes off en roll down de hill so dey could see dat you didn't
hab no bones broken, er sores on yer. (I wouldin' tek mine off). Ef
nobody bid on you, you wuz tuk ter de slave mart en sold. I wuz sold
dere. A bunch ob dem wuz sent ter Mississippi en dey had dere ankles
fas' end tergedder en dey had ter walk w'iles de tradahs rid.

W'en I wuz sold ter marster Simpkins, mah second mistress
made me a house slave en I wuked only at de big house en mah wuk
wus ter nuss en dress de chilluns en he'ps mah missis in her dressin'.

De young slaves wuz hired out ter nuss de white chilluns. I wuz
hired as nuss girl at seven y'ars ole en started cookin' at ten.
I nebber had a chance ter go ter schul.

I'm de mammy ob 14 chilluns, seven boys en seven gals. I wuz
next ter de olest ob four chillun. Mah missis useter hire me out
ter hotels en taverns.

Sum marsters fed dere slaves meat en sum wouldin' let dem hab
a bite. One marster we useter 'yer 'bout would grease his slaves
mouth on Sunday mawnin', en tell dem ef any body axed ef dey had
meat ter say "yes, lots ob hit".

W'en dey got ready ter whup dem dey'd put dem down on a pit
widout any clothes, stand back wid a bull whip en cut de blood out.
I member de niggers would run 'way en hide out.

De only fun de young folks had wuz w'en de ole folks had
a quiltin'. W'ile de ole folks wuz wukin' on de quilt de young
ones would git in 'nuther room, dance en hab a good time. Dey'd
hab a pot turned down at de do'er ter keep de white folks fum
'yearin' dem. De white folks didn't want us ter l'arn nothin' en ef
a slave picked up a lettle piece ob papah, dey would yell "put dat down
you - you wan't ter git in our business."

De white folks wouldin' let de slaves pray, ef dey got ter pray
hit wus w'iles walkin' 'hind de plow. White folks would whup de
slaves ef dey 'yeard dem sing er pray.

I wuz a big girl w'en dey build de Capitol. I played on de
hill 'fore hit wuz built en I toted blocks fum dere w'en hit wuz

bein' built. I wuz livin' in Dickson County w'en Fort Donelson
Wuz tuk. I seed de fust gun boat dat kum up de Cumberland River.
I wuz standin' in de Do'er w'en I se'd hit kumin', but hit didn't
tek me long ter git back in de back ob de house. I wuz skeered
dey would shoot.

Mah marster run a fer'y en atter de gun boat kum up de riber,
he got skeered en gib mah ole man de fer'y, en w'en de soldiers
kum ter tek Fort Negley he set dem 'cross de river.

A man at Ashland City dat made whisk'y would hab Mr. Simpkins
bring a load ob logs up ter Ashland City en den bring a load ob
whiskey down en hide hit so de Yankees would'nt git hit.

Mah marster had a fish trap at de mouth ob Harper en w'en de
gun boat passed dey shot thro' de trap.

I wuz right 'yer w'en de Civil wah wuz gwin on, en de soldiers
wuz dressed up en beatin' de drums.

No honey, we didn't git nothin' w'en we wuz freed. Jes druv
'way widout nothin' ter do wid. We got in a waggin en druv ter
nuther man's plantashun. Mah ole man made a crap dere. Sum ob de
slaves might hab got sump'in but I dunno nobody dat did. I wuz
skeered ter op'n mah do'er atter dark on 'count ob Ku Klux Klan,
dey wuz red hot.

I member w'en de sta'rs fell. I wuz small but de ole folks run
out en loked at dem, kum back set down en cried, dey thop hit
me'nt de worl' wuz kumin' ter an end.

De peeple wuz skeered w'en dey se'd de comet wid de long tail.
Dey thoet hit wuz a sign ob wah.

I'se cooked eve'y since I wuz freed. I stayed in Henry Galbles
kitchen five long y'ars, en since I'se had dese strokes hit's broke
me up 'till I kin do nothin'. I 'long ter de Methodist Church. I

think de young peeples ez turrible, en dis white en black mar'iags not be 'lowed.

De songs I member ez:

" Dark wuz de Night".

" Good Ole Daniel".

I'se nebber voted but I'se electioneered fer dem. Hab nebber had any frens in office.

I wuz 'yer w'en Henry Clay en James K. Polk wuz runnin'. I wuz hired at de ole City Hotel ovuh on de river. I wuz din'in room servant dere. Mah marster would hab me sing a song fer him 'bout de Democrats. "Hooray de kuntry ez risin'; rise up en drown ole Clay en his pizen." I guess ole Clay wuz a right good fellow but he played cards wid de niggers in de cellar.

De only thing I 'ember 'bout de 'structshun time wuz sum ob de whites didn't wan' de niggers ter vote.

I stays 'yer wid mah daughter. Dat ez de only support I hab since I had deze strokes en bin unable ter do fer mahse'f.

Ex-Slave Stories

Subject: Joseph Leonidas Star,# I33 Quebec Place, Knoxville,Tennessee

If the poetic strain in the Dunbar Negroes of the south is an inheri-
tance and not " just a gift from On High! Knoxville,Tennessee's aged Negro
Poet,-born Joseph Leonidas Star,-but prominently known in the community as
"Lee" Star,Poet,Politician and Lodge Man,-thinks that Georgia's poetic genius
Paul Lawrence Dunbar,"maybe took his writin' spells" from him.

" My grandfather and Paul Lawrence Dunbar's grandfather was cousins.
He were a much younger man than I am, for I was eighty-one years old the
twenty-sixth of December,1937. So I reckon I give it down to my kin-man. But
it seem to me,that Poets is just born thataway. Po'try is nothin' but Truth
anyway, and it's Truth was sets us free. And that makes me a free-born citizen
bothways and every ways. I were born free. I were always happy-natured and I
expect to die thataway. One of my poems is named,"Be Satisfied!' and I say in
it that if a man's got somethin' to eat, and teeth to bite, he should be
satisfied. You cant take your good/with you. Old man Rockefeller,when he died
here awhile back, went away from here 'thout his hat and shoes. That's the way
its goin' to be with all us, no matter what our color is."

"The people 'round here calls me "Lee" Star, and I want to tell you,
Lee Star is a free-born man. But of course, things bein' as they were,both
my mother and father were slaves.That is for a few years. They lived in
Greenville,Tennessee. My mother,Maria Guess, was free'd before the emancipation,
by the good words of her young white mistress, who told ' me all when she was
about to die, she wanted ' em to set Maria free, 'cause she didnt want her
little playmate to be nobodys else's slave.They was playmates you see.My mother
was eleven years old when she was freed."

" When she was about fourteen and my father Henry Dunbar wanted to marry he had to first buy his freedom.In them times a slave couldnt marry a free'd person. So he bought his freedom from his Marster LLoyd Bullen, and a good friend of Andrew Johnson,the presi-dent. My father an' him was friends too. So he bought his freedom, for just a little of somethin' I disremember what,' cause they didnt aim to make him buy his freedom high. He made good money though.He was a carpenter, blacksmith, shoe maker and knowed a lot more trades. His Master was broadhearted, and good to his slaves, and he let 'em work at anything they want to, when they was done their part of white folks chore-work."

" Both my father and mother was learned in the shoe makin' trade. "hen they come to Knoxville to live, and where I was born, they had a great big shoe shop out there close to where Governor Brownlow lived. Knoxville just had three streets,two runnin'east and west and one run north and south. I well remember when General Burnside come to Knoxville.That was endurin' the siege of Knoxville. Before he marched his men out to the Battle of Fort Saunders, he stopped his solider band in front of our shoe shop and serenaded my mother and father. I was a little boy and I climed up on the porch bannisters and sat there and lissen' to that music."

" I remember another big man come here once when I was a boy and I served the transient trade at a little eatin' place right where the Atkin Ho-tel is now. Jeff Davis come there to eat, when he stopped over between trains.That was in 1869. No, I disremember what he eat or how he behave.He didnt seem no different from any other man.He was nince lookin' wore a long tail coat and his boots was plenty blacked.He favored pictures of Abraham Lincoln."as about middle-height and had short,dark chin-whiskers. I were very busy at the time,an' if they was any excitement I didnt know it."

Joseph Leonadis Star.

"Yes, I've seen many a slave in my day. One of my boy playmates was a
slave child. His name is Sam Rogan and he lives now at the County Poor Farm.
I make it a point not to dwell too much on slave times. I was learned different.
I've had considerable schoolin', went to my first school in the old First
Presbyterian church. My teachers was white folks from the North. They give us
our education and give us clothes and things sent down here from the North.
That was just after the surrender. I did see a terrible sight once. A slave
with chains on him as long as from here to the street. He was in an ole' buggy,
settin' between two white men and they was passin' through Knoxville. My mother
and father wouldnt lissen' to me tell' em about it when I got home. And I hope
I forget everything I ever knowed or heard about salves, and slave times."

Joseph Leonidas Star, no longer works at the shoemakers trade. He
writes poetry poetry and lives leisurely in a three room frame shanty, in a
row of shabbier ones that face each other disconsolately on a typical negro
alleyway, that has no shade trees and no paveing. "Lee's" house is the only
one that does not wabble uneasily, flush with the muddy alley. His stands
on a small brick foundation, a few feet behind a private xxxxxx hedge in front,
with a brick wall along the side in which he has cemented a few huge conch
shells.

After fifty-four years residence here, a political boss in his ward,
and the only Negro member of the Young White Men's Republican League, Star's
influence in his community is attested by the fact that when he "destructed",
the Knoxville City Council to "please do somethin' about it, Knoxville being
too big a city to keep callin' street's alleys, the City Council promptly and
unanimously voted to change the name of King's xxxx Alley to Quebec xxxxxx
Place.

Joseph Leonidas Star.

When the interviewer called, Star's door was padlocked. But he appeared

soon, having received word by the grape-vine system that   some one " was to

see him", -"They told me it was the Sherriff" he laughed. He came down the

long muddy alley at a lively clip. He claims he is able to walk about 20 miles

each day, just to keep in condition. He wore a broad-brimmed black"derby-hat",

a neatly pressed serge suit in two tones, a soiled white pleated shirt and a

frazzled-edged black bow tie. His coat lapels and vest-front were adorned with

badges and emblems, including his Masonic pins, a Friendship Medal, his Republi-

can button and a silve r crucifix. The Catholic church, according to Lee, is

the only one in Knoxville which permits the black man to worship under the same

roof with his white brothers.

Many of Star's poems have been published in the local and state papers.

He keeps a record of deaths of all citizens, and has done so for sixty years.

He calls the one, which records murders and hanging, his "Doomsday Book",

and" encoached" in it he claims is an accurate date record of all such events of

importance in his lifetime. His records are neatly inscribed in a printing

form and very legible. His conversation is marked by grammatical incongruities,

but he does not speak the negro dialect.

INTERVIEW

DAN THOMAS

941 Jefferson Street

Nashville, Tennessee

"I wuz bawn in slavery in 1847 at Memphis, Tennessee en mah marster wuz Deacon Allays. Mah mammy wuz de cook at de big house. Mah mammy d'ed soon atter I wuz bawn, en de Missis had me raised on a bottle. Marster en Missis treatus all dere slaves kindly en plenty ter eat en eve'y one wuz happy. I dunno nuthin 'bout mah daddy er whar he went. I hab no kin in dis worl'. All I eber yeard wuz dat all mah folks kum fum Africa. Mah Missis would tell me dat I mus' be good en mine en eberbody will lak' you en ef she d'ed, dey would tek keer ob me. Dat ez w'at dey hab don."

"I wuked 'round de house 'tel I wuz 'bout ten y'ars ole en de Marster put me ter wuk in his big whiskey house. W'en I got 'bout 21 y'ars ole, I would go out ter collect bills fum Marster's customers en hit tuk me 'bout a week ter git all 'round. I wuzn't 'lowed ter tek money but had ter git dere checks. I also wuked 18 y'ars as bar tender. Marster en Mistress d'ed 'bout four y'ars 'fore whiskey went out ob de United States. I stay wid dem 'til dey d'ed."

"Atter de Marster en Missis d'ed de doctor sezs I would hab ter leave Memphis on 'count ob my health. I kum ter Nashville en got a job at de "Powder Plant" durin' de Worl' War, en stayed dere 'til hit wuz ovuh. I den gets wuk at Foster en Creighton in Nashville 'till dey tole me dat I wuz too ole ter wuk. I makes mah livin' now by haulin' slop en pickin' up things dat de

white folks throw in dere trash pile en sum ob hit I sell ter
de papah en junk dealers. De white peeple he'p me now also."

"I se'd dem sell a lot ob slaves in Mississippi, jes' lak
hosses en hogs, one time w'en de Marster en Mistress made a
trip down dere. Lots ob times dey made trips 'round de kuntry
en dey allus tuk me 'long. I se'd sum cru'l Marsters dat hitched
up dere slaves ter plows en made dem plow lak hosses en mules did."

"Atter de slaves got dere freedum, dey had ter look atter
demselves so dey would wuk on plantations till dey got so dey
could rent a place, lak you rent houses en farms terday. Sum
got places whar dey wuk'd fer wages."

"I voted three times in mah life but lawdy dat wuz a long
time ago. I voted fer Teddy Roosevelt en Woodrow Wilson, en
mah last vote wuz 'bout two y'ars pas'."

"Hab no tales handed down by mah peeple. W'en I would
try ter git info'mation, atter I got o'ler, all dey would say
wuz, "You wuz raised on a bottle en hab no peeple ob you own."

"Oh mah goodness! Hit jes par'lises me ter see how dem
young peeple ez doin' terday. Lawdy hab mercy but dere ez as
much diff'ent fum ole times as day en nite en hit looks lak
things hab gone astray. Wuz tole lots 'bout de Ku Klux Klan
en how dey would catch en whup de cul'ed peeple, but mah white
folks made me stay in en dey neber got me."

"I member seein' Andrew Jackson, General Grant en Abraham
Lincoln, member seein' General Andrew Jackson git'in ready
fer war by marchin' his soldiers erroun'. I se'd 'im ride his
big white hoss up en down ter see how dey marched."

"One song I lack'd best ob all wuz, 'Mah Ole Mammy ez De'd
en Gon',' 'Let me Sit B'neath de Willow Tree.' Don't member
uther songs now."

INTERVIEW

Sylvia Watkins

411 14th Avenue N.

Nashville, Tennessee.

I'se said ter be 91 y'ars ole. I wuz young w'en de War wuz goin' on. I wuz bawn in Bedford County. Mah mammy wuz named Mariah. She had six chillun by mah daddy en three by her fust husban.

Mah missis wuz named Emily Hatchet en de young missises wuz Mittie en Bettie, dey wuz twins. We had good clothes ter w'ar en w'en we went ter de table hit wuz loaded wid good food en we could set down en eat our stomachs full. Oh Lawd I wish dem days wuz now so I'd hab sum good food. Ob course, we had ter wuk in de fiel's en mek w'at we et.

W'en we'd finish our day's wuk our missis would let us go out en play hide en seek, Puss in de corner, en diff'ent games.

Mah mammy wuz sold in Virginia w'en she wuz a gurl. She sezs 'bou 60 ob em wuz put in de road en druv down 'yer by a slave trader, lak a bunch ob cattle. Mah mammy en two ob mah sistahs wuz put on a block, sold en carried ter Alabama. We nebor 'yeard fum dem nomo', en dunno whar dey ez.

I wuz willed ter mah young missis w'en she ma'ried. I wuz young en, ob course, she whuped me, but she wasn't mean ter me. I needed eve'y whupin' she eber gib me, cause I wuz allus fightin'. Mah missis allus called me her little nig.

Mah daddy could only see mah mammy Wednesday en Saturday nites, en ef'n he kum wid'out a pass de pat-rollers would whup 'im er run 'im 'til his tongue hung out. On dem nites we would sit up en look fer daddy en lots ob times he wuz out ob bref cose he had run so much.

Mah white folks had a loom en we wove our own clothes. I wuz nuss en house girl en l'arned how ter sew en nit. Mah young missis wuz

blind 'fore she died. I useter visit her once a Ye'r en she'd load
me down wid things ter tek home, a linsey petticoat, ham bones, cracklins
en diff'ent things. She died 18 years ago almos' a 100 ye'r ole.

De white folks wouldn't let de slaves hab a book er papah fer fear
dey'd l'arn sumpin', en ef dey wan'ed ter pray dey'd tu'n a kettle down
at dere cabin do'er. I member fearin' mah mammy pray "Oh Father op'n
up de do'ers en sho us lite." I'd look up ter de ceiling ter see ef
he wuz gonna op'n up sumpin'; silly, silly me, thinkin' such. I's
'longs ter de Missionary Baptist chuch but I don't git ter go very off'n.

I wuz tole 'fore freedum dat de slaves would git a mule, land en
a new suit, but our missis didn't gib us a thing. She promis' me, mah
br'rer, en three sistahs ef'n we would stay wid her a ye'r, en he'p
her mek a crop she would gib us sump'in ter start us a crop on w'en
we lef' her.

Mah daddy's marster wus named Bob Rankin, he gib mah daddy a hog,
sum chickens, let him hab a cow ter milk en land ter raise a crop on.
He wan'ed mah daddy ter git us tergedder ter he'p daddy raise a crop
but since mah missis had promised us so much, daddy let us stay wid
her a ye'r. On de nite mah daddy kum fer us, mah missis sezs I've not
got nuthin ter gib you, fer I won't hab nobody ter do nuthin fer me.
We went wid our daddy. We lived dere on Marster Rankin's farm fer
ye'rs in fact so long we tho't de place 'longed ter mah daddy. We
had a house wid big cracks in hit, had a big fier place, a big pot dat
hong on de fier en a skillet dat we cooked corn bread in. Had a hill
ob taters under de house, would raise up a plank, rake down in de dirt
git taters, put dem in de fier ter roast. We had meat ter eat in de
middle ob de day but none at mawnin' er nite. We got one pair ob shoes
a ye'r, dey had brass on de toes. I uster git out en shine de toes
ob mine, we called hit gol' on our shoes. We wuked in de fiel' wid
mah daddy, en I know how ter do eberting dere ez ter do in a fiel'
cept plow, I wuz allus ter slender ter hold a plow. We had grease

lamps. A thing lak a goose neck wid platted rag wick in hit. Would put grease in hit.

Durin' slavery if one marster had a big boy en 'nuther had a big gal de marsters made dem libe tergedder. Ef'n de 'oman didn't hab any chilluns, she wuz put on de block en sold en 'nuther 'oman bought. You see dey raised de chilluns ter mek money on jes lak we raise pigs ter sell.

Mah mammy tole me 'bout de sta'rs fallin' en den I se'ed de second fallin' ob sta'rs. Dey didn't hit de groun' lak de fust did. I member de comet hit had a long tail. I lef' mah daddy en kum ter Nashville wid missis Nellie Rankin, (daddy's young missus(in 1882; hab bin 'yer eber since. I'se dun house wuk fer a lot ob peeples. Kep house fer a 'oman in Belle Meade fer 14 ye'rs. Now I'se aint able ter do nothin. I'se bin ma'ried twice. Ma'ried Jimm Ferguson, libed wid 'im 20 ye'ars he d'ed. Two ye'ars later I mar'ed George Watkins, lived wid him 8 ye'ars; two ye'ars ago he died. I'se neber had any chilluns. I kep wan'in ter 'dopt a lettle gal, de fust husban' wouldn't do hit. 'Bout 5½ ye'ars ago de second husban' George kum in wid a tiny baby, sezs 'yer ez a boy baby I 'dopted. I sezs dat ez you wown baby cose hits jes like yer. He denied hit, but eben now de boy ez e'zackly lak George. He's six ye'rs ole en gwine ter school. I'se got mah hands full tryin' ter raise 'im 'lone. W'en George died he had a small inshorance policy. I paid mah taxes, I owns dis home, en bought mahself three hogs. I sold two en kilt one. Den I got three mor' jes' a short time ago. Sum kind ob zeeze got among dem en dey all d'ed.

Yas I'se voted four er five times, but neber had any frens in office. I don' think dis white-black mar'iage should be 'lowed. Dey should be whupped wid a bull whup.

As far as I know de ex-slaves hab wuked at diff'ent kins ob jobs en now sum I know ez in de po-house, sum git' in belief order en urthers ez lak mahself, hab dere homes en gettin' 'long bes' dey kin. I needs milk en cod liver oil fer dis lettle boy but can't buy it.

I dunno nothin' 'bout slave uprisin's. De songs I member ez:

"All Gawds Chilluns up Yonder,"

"I want ter Shout Salvation."

"Down by de River Side."

INTERVIEW

NARCISSUS YOUNG

Rear 532 1st Street No.

Nashville, Tennessee

"I'se 96 y'ars ole. Bawn in slavery en mah marster
wuz Isham Lamb en mah missis wuz Martha Lamb. Mah mammy
d'ed w'en I wuz three y'ars ole en I wuz raised in de
house 'til I wuz big 'nuff ter wuk out in de fiels wid de
uthers. Mah missis l'arn me ter sew, weav en spin. I also
he'lped ter cook en wuk in de house. Atter I got big'er I
went ter chuch wid mah white folks en had ter set wid urther
slaves in dat part ob de chuch whar nobody but slaves would
be 'lowed. In slavery I'se git no money fer wuk'n but I don'
steal as mah white folks sho gib me en de uther slaves plenty
good things ter eat. Clothes good 'nuff fer anybody, candy, en
we went ter parties en urther places, en w'at else could I'se
wan'?"

"Mah missis l'arned me ter pray, "Now I lay me down ter
sleep. I pray de Lawd mah soul ter keep, but if I should
die 'fore I wake, I pray de Lawd mah soul ter tek." I jined
de Primitive Baptist Chuch w'ile young en b'en dere ebe'y since."

"I member de ole song back dere, "Rock a Bye Baby, Yo Daddy's
gon' a Huntin' ter git a Rabbit Skin ter put de Baby in.""

"I wuz whup'd by mah missis fer things dat I ought'n dun,
but dat wuz rite. De hahdest whup'in she eber gib me wuz 'bout
two hen aigs. I had gathured de aigs in a bucket en tuk dem ter
de house en I se'd de big fier in de fier-place so I tuk out two
ob de aigs en put dem in de hot ashes ter bake. Mah missis se'd

de aigs en axed who put dem dere. I tole her I didunt do hit,
but she knowed I did. So she tole me she don' keer 'bout de
two aigs, but dat she wuz gwine ter whup me fer tellin' a lie.
Dey don't raise chilluns lak dat now."

"I don't b'leeve in Niggers en whites ma'rin' en I wuz
raised by de "quality" en I'se b'leeves eber one should ma'rie
in dere culor."

"I think de young peeples ob ter day ez dogs en sluts, en
yer kin guess de rest."

"One day 'bout 12 o'clock we se'd de Yankee soldiers pas'
our house. De missus hid her fine things, but dey don' kum on
de place. All us Niggers run ter de cellar en hid. We found
de sugah barrels en we scracht 'round fer sum sugah ter eat."

"One time de Ku Klux Klan kum ter our house but dey harm
nobody. Guess day wuz lookin' fer sum slave er sum one fum
'nother plantation widout dere marster's pass."

"I se'd a lot ob sta'rs fall one time but dey neber teched
de groun'. En I members seein' a comet wid a long bright shinin'
tail."

"Atter freedum all de slaves lef' de plantation but I
stayed dere a long time. I kum ter Nashville ovah thurty
y'ars ago en I'se wuk'd as cook en house. wuk'r twenty y'ars fer
one party; eleben y'ars fer 'nother, en menny y'ars fer 'nother.
I knows you won't b'leeve me but at one time I weigh ovuh 400
pounds, but now I'm nothin' but skin en bon'. (She weighs at
least 200 pounds now). I bekum feeble en couldn't wuk out,
en eber since den I'se bin kum' up a mountain, but now I git he'ps
by de Social Security.

TITLES IN THE

SLAVE NARRATIVES SERIES

FROM APPLEWOOD BOOKS

ALABAMA SLAVE NARRATIVES
ISBN 1-55709-010-6 • $14.95
Paperback • 7-1/2" x 9-1/4" • 168 pp

ARKANSAS SLAVE NARRATIVES
ISBN 1-55709-011-4 • $14.95
Paperback • 7-1/2" x 9-1/4" • 172 pp

FLORIDA SLAVE NARRATIVES
ISBN 1-55709-012-2 • $14.95
Paperback • 7-1/2" x 9-1/4" • 168 pp

GEORGIA SLAVE NARRATIVES
ISBN 1-55709-013-0 • $14.95
Paperback • 7-1/2" x 9-1/4" • 172 pp

INDIANA SLAVE NARRATIVES
ISBN 1-55709-014-9 • $14.95
Paperback • 7-1/2" x 9-1/4" • 140 pp

KENTUCKY SLAVE NARRATIVES
ISBN 1-55709-016-5 • $14.95
Paperback • 7-1/2" x 9-1/4" • 136 pp

MARYLAND SLAVE NARRATIVES
ISBN 1-55709-017-3 • $14.95
Paperback • 7-1/2" x 9-1/4" • 88 pp

MISSISSIPPI SLAVE NARRATIVES
ISBN 1-55709-018-1 • $14.95
Paperback • 7-1/2" x 9-1/4" • 184 pp

MISSOURI SLAVE NARRATIVES
ISBN 1-55709-019-X • $14.95
Paperback • 7-1/2" x 9-1/4" • 172 pp

NORTH CAROLINA SLAVE NARRATIVES
ISBN 1-55709-020-3 • $14.95
Paperback • 7-1/2" x 9-1/4" • 168 pp

OHIO SLAVE NARRATIVES
ISBN 1-55709-021-1 • $14.95
Paperback • 7-1/2" x 9-1/4" • 128 pp

OKLAHOMA SLAVE NARRATIVES
ISBN 1-55709-022-X • $14.95
Paperback • 7-1/2" x 9-1/4" • 172 pp

SOUTH CAROLINA SLAVE NARRATIVES
1-55709-023-8 • $14.95
Paperback • 7-1/2" x 9-1/4" • 172 pp

TENNESSEE SLAVE NARRATIVES
ISBN 1-55709-024-6 • $14.95
Paperback • 7-1/2" x 9-1/4" • 92 pp

VIRGINIA SLAVE NARRATIVES
ISBN 1-55709-025-4 • $14.95
Paperback • 7-1/2" x 9-1/4" • 68 pp

* * * * * * * * * * * * * * *

IN THEIR VOICES: SLAVE NARRATIVES
A companion CD of original recordings
made by the Federal Writers' Project.
Former slaves from many states tell
stories, sing long-remembered songs,
and recall the era of American slavery.
This invaluable treasure trove of oral
history, through the power of voices of
those now gone, brings back to life the
people who lived in slavery.
ISBN 1-55709-026-2 • $19.95
Audio CD

* * * * * * * * * * * * * * *

TO ORDER, CALL 800-277-5312 OR
VISIT US ON THE WEB AT WWW.AWB.COM

CPSIA information can be obtained
at www.ICGtesting.com
Printed in the USA
BVHW010628180620
581747BV00014B/538

9 781557 090249